# The Obsidian Chronicles Trilogy

## (Minecraft Adventure Short Stories)

### By Mark Mulle

PUBLISHED BY:

Mark Mulle

# TABLE OF CONTENTS

# Ender Rain

I live in a world not at all like your own.

In this world, there are four essential places. The Green is the places above ground, the places where trees and grass grow, where mountains rise up, the places where cows might moo woefully, waiting for a purpose in their lives. We live in the Green.

There is the Underground, all places which must be reached from caves or mine shafts or great rifts in the ground. These are the places where the sun does not and never has touched, where the creatures of story and legend are said to roam.

There is the Nether, a horrible, blasted landscape overrun by fire and the beasts that embody it, where infernal castles and strongholds dot the maps which never are finished. This place must be reached from a certain archway made of black stone, anointed with a drop of blood and burned.

There is the End, from which no man has ever returned. There are legends that talk of a grand gate somewhere in the Green that pulsates with an acrid energy, which can only be seen by the stricken eyes of the already-dead. Nobody knows what is there.

It is the Green which enriches our lives, of course, but we are an industrious people. We cannot survive on sunshine alone. Thus, we began one day long ago our descent into the Underground, to find the treasures that it had to offer us

Those are the stories we tell here, at least. Really the Green is just as fraught with danger and hardship as anywhere else. At night, when the sun sets and it becomes dark, things come to terrorize the villages. Hordes of the walking dead, their acrid flesh just barely hanging onto their bones or perhaps already fallen completely off and shed behind. Giant spiders the size of horses that climb the sides of your house and stare at you with their glowing red eyes through your windows. tall, thin figures in black, with burning purple eyes that slowly deconstruct your house before you.

And in order to protect yourself from these creatures, you must build shelters. The first, early shelters, made out of packed earth, were enough, but they soon began to fall apart, dry out and crumble. The monsters took that opportunity to do what they did best. We tried building from wood, and it held well until the first big storm. We were not prepared for the lightning, for the fires that ensued.

We started to build our houses out of small stones held together with mud and mortar. These sort of cobbled-stone houses are still very solid and reliable, but some of us cannot help but wish for something stronger than just bricks of mud and pebbles. To get stronger materials, one must look underground.

Deep underground, in the twisting cave systems, we discovered an abundant supply of iron ore, which could be smelted to bring out the metallic bits and get rid of imperfections. This was the beginning of the first real economy where we were. There were those that went down into the earth to get the metal, and there were those who formed it into tools on the surface. My name is Vincent, and I was a miner, as was Mary, as was James. Austin, Katy, and Anna were the crafters. They generally stayed on the Green, using the resources we would get them.

Austin decided one day that he wanted to come down into the earth with us, so he and I partnered up, and descended the long mine shaft. Already, breaking into the deep caverns far below from above ground had been laborious, but now that we had established the route, it was a breeze and his enthusiasm was resurfacing.

"I wonder what else could be this far down in the earth," he said.

"We've found all kinds of ores down here. Plenty of coal to keep your furnaces burning, plenty of iron to keep building, even some gold. Gold comes up out of the ground like butter, it's so soft." I shrugged the stack of pickaxes higher up on my shoulder.

"And jewels? What of those?"

"Deep blue ones and glittering glass-like ones and stark green ones. They come about more seldom, but they are also here."

He rubbed his hands together. "Here, give me one of those picks," he said, and I shouldered him one made of iron, fresh out of the forges only yesterday.

We worked together, side-by-side, opening a long tunnel in the ground dozens of meters down. Onward and onward we pressed in the stone, crumbling it around us as we kept on.

"The funny thing is," Austin was saying, "I have an inkling that there's something I once heard about, a stone stronger than iron, black and smooth, down this far. It's dangerous to get it, though, because it's always—" His pickaxe struck into a piece of stone, pulled it free, and the hallway rumbled around us.

My eyes grew wide. This was the death that miners feared the most, a collapse in a tunnel. Even with these picks, we'd be trapped. The loose stone and gravel and sand would slowly settle into an impenetrable wall, and no matter how much we cleared, there would be more to fall down and take its place. I could feel my blood pressure rise.

Austin, too, felt the tension grow, and his knuckles turned white on the handle. "What—"

"We need to reinforce this bit of the tunnel. Let's get those wood supports up," I said quietly. "This happens, but it is always best to make sure the tunnel is safe." Austin cracked his knuckles, never a coward but wise enough to take safety precautions, and he opened up his bag.

We spent the next small while making sure that the tunnel would not collapse, propping up the sides and roof of the cavern with stout wooden beams. Even with the supports there, though, something felt off. I had to shrug it off, put it to imagination. After all, we'd made sure to—

The sudden crunching of stone breaking apart, of a ton of gravel and dirt suddenly pouring down in a torrent, struck me in the ears, and I had barely enough time to turn and see Austin get bowled over by the flow of rock, quickly being engulfed by the heavy death that took no prisoners.

"Austin!" I spat, and before the flow had even stopped I had flung the planks aside and seized the broad, flat shovel leaning on the wall, beginning to fling the debris behind me in a desperate attempt to reach my compatriot before he was crushed, before the fine dust crept into his lungs and rendered him no more than wet dirt himself.

"Austin! Hold on! I'm going to get you out!" I cried, my eyes dirty with soot and dust, my mouth full of fine stone.

I saw a slight shifting in the stone, like something straining underneath it, and attacked with fervor until I unearthed a patch of cloth, Austin's red jacket. Discarding the shovel, I moved the rocks away with my bare hands, feeling the shards ripping into my skin. Austin heaved himself free from the pile, and lurched onto his back, heaving and coughing.

He spit blood and wet dust from his mouth, wiped his eyes with his sleeve, and breathed.

"This job sucks, and you can have it back," he coughed.

I sighed my relief. Thank the stars we didn't just lose him. A laugh rose up in my gut, and we both sat in the gloom and dust and dark laughing for the next several minutes.

Back up in the main house on the Green, Austin leaned back on his bed, and drank from his bowl of soup. "Man, it was crazy!" He gestured with his spoon. "We thought we were safe, but then the whole tunnel came down on me! It was this huge sudden torrent, and I got bowled over and buried!" He drank again, and the others listened. "And the whole time, all I could think was, 'I absolutely will not sand for this!'"

Silence shook the very air as we all stared at him for a second. Anne was the first to speak up.

"I hate you so much," she said, and we all laughed. Back up in the house, we were all safe, and Austin was largely recovered from his encounter with the fingers of the deep earth. We lost some of the materials we'd collected, of course, but somehow I could not help but think it was worth not losing one of our people. Austin even seemed to be taking near-death at the hands of the Underground very well, in stride.

I did not know what he was planning.

It was mid-day the next day. We took every couple of days off from mining so that we didn't get stir crazy and claustrophobic, so I was up in the farmyard helping Mary build what she was calling "the greatest pig sanctuary in the entire world" when I saw Austin come up out of the mine shaft, carrying an obviously empty bag and looking pleased with himself.

"Hey, man!" I called, and waved him over. As he approached, I noticed the distinct smell of salt peter coming from him. "What are you up to? We don't mine today; it's the day off."

Austin smiled, showed me the bag. "I'm getting a little self-satisfactory revenge," he said, and just as he did so, the ground shook like an earthquake, and a huge gout of dust issued from the mouth of the mine shaft.

It was over just as quickly as it started, and as the shaking stopped, I knew exactly what he had done.

"You blew up the mine? You blew up the mine."

"Think of it as payback."

"Dude, the Underground doesn't have feelings to hurt, and even if it did, it is massive! It would not even notice a little tunnel caving in from an explosion. And where did you get the explosives for this?"

"We had a store of gunpowder from the big green monsters that we manage to pick off sometimes. I just applied a bit of science."

"You . . . you must be mad."

He grinned. "But it was so satisfying."

He volunteered to go with us to look at the damage he had caused in the tunnel, probably out of a sense of curiosity as to how much carnage his explosives wreaked, so we all geared up to excavate. The six of us descended carefully, ropes and picks at the ready in case something happened. The closer we got to the place Austin had been trapped, the more dust covered the floor and walls.

The epicenter of the blast was surrounded by a space void of stone in a rough sphere some twenty meters across. It seemed as though much of the rubble had been vaporized by the blast, and the exposed stone now was rough and unworked. Austin whistled and then hopped into the bottom of this crater. He tapped on some stone with his pick.

"And to top it all off," he said with a grin, "I found us some diamonds!" He knocked the glittering jewel free from the stone with the butt of his pick but then lost his footing as the ground under him crumbled a bit too. A hole opened up beneath him, and he tumbled into the dark.

Rushing to the edge of the hole, ready to start saving Austin yet again, I instead saw a tunnel, one lit by what must have been ancient lamps still burning. Austin sat wide-eyed on a rail cart track that stretched both directions down the tunnel, which was reinforced much in the same way we reinforced our own.

"We are the only ones on this continent, right? That was the deal, right?" James paced back and forth. We reinforced our doors that night, and everyone gathered up on the second floor from the sudden paranoia wave.

Katy cut up bread, put thick slices with butter on the edge of the bowls of mushroom soup. "Has anyone else found any traces of others besides us?"

"Not a single one. We're here alone," I said, my eyes falling first on the staircase, then on the frames on the walls full of swords and axes.

Mary shook her head. "Lots of animal life but no human to my eyes."

"I've got nothing." Austin shifted on the chest he had taken as a seat.

Anne was silent, contemplating. We all looked at her, and she furrowed her brows. "I cannot be sure of it, but when I was out in the jungle when we first came, before I had my bearings, I got really lost. We were all looking for a good place to settle, so I figured getting lost wasn't a terrible thing. Anyway, deep in the jungle, just as it was getting dark, I thought I saw through the trees a big structure of some sort. It was too dark to see, but it looked like it was something built—not naturally formed."

Austin's ears perked up. "Why didn't you tell us before?" he questioned.

She shrugged. "I thought it was just a trick of the light through the trees. Now I'm not so sure."

We sat in silence, contemplating the meaning of such possible evidence of others here. I sucked a deep breath and stood up. "Well, here's how I see it. We are the only ones here now. Nobody has seen anyone else, just the signs that they were here at some point."

James, who had gone pale white at the realization, quietly interjected. "No, we see them all the time. At night. When it is dark, and they come out of their hiding places."

No way, I thought. The monsters that plagued our nights before we had strong walls?

"It's true," Katy began, "that these monsters look vaguely like humans and walk on two legs like humans, but what evidence—"

"Evidence? Some of them wear leather clothes, some of them carry with them old tools, and some of them drop scraps of fresh food when they die! These creatures . . . they are the remains of the people who were once here! They have to be . . ." James trailed off.

"Okay, putting this all together," I said and counted off on my fingers. "We're not alone here. Others were here before, but they are not any longer. We have found the evidence of this previous occupation. We also think that the skeletons and zombies that come out at night may be the remains of said previous population. Here's what I think now. If they built big structures and mineshafts and the like, then they might have left things in those places, and since they are no longer using them, should we accidentally stumble across them, it would not be against any rules to take those things, right?"

Mary glowered at me. "Grave-robbing?"

"Not grave-robbing, no. These would not be graves. If we found a gravesite, it would be different; we leave that alone. I mean like old houses or the like, storerooms in the mines."

Austin and James seemed interested. Even Katy looked like she was contemplating it. Anne shook her head though and sighed.

"If you four want to traipse through the ruins of a long-gone people, then feel free, but I might stay out of there. I am not comfortable going into potentially zombie-infested city blocks." Mary nodded her agreement, and that seemed to be that.

"It's settled, then. Tomorrow, we'll try to explore some of that underground mine, see where it leads."

That night was tense, knowing that the things that stalked in the dark outside might have very well been just like us, huddled in a house sometime in the past.

The next day, four of us stood at the entrance to the tunnel we'd found. We would treat it just like any other tunnel we would explore, except this one was already at least partially lit and dug out. In we went, pickaxes and ropes and bags at the ready.

The tunnel was some five or six meters wide, and about three or four tall, and it stretched in both directions. We decided to go eastward first, and, marking on the stone walls as we went, our trek began.

What followed was a labyrinthine mass of twists and turns, wooden supports partially decayed and portions of the tunnel filled with water that had leaked in over several years. Here and there just out of sight someone would hear something or catch a glimpse of movement, but we never saw anything fully, until . . .

I turned a corner and was suddenly faced with a literal ton of spider webs, from the floor to the ceiling, stretching to both walls and positively filling up the entire tunnel for at least the two meters I could see through it. The webs were so thick; I don't think we could have gone through them without lighting them on fire. I tried to step back, but James turned the corner just at that time. His frame pushed mine face-first into the webs. I started to fall, but the sticky silk kept me standing.

Of course, it also immediately wrapped around my legs and arms, sticking and tangling like spider webs are wont to do, and I found myself struggling and getting stuck further into them. James seized the back of my collar and tried to haul me out, but the sticky threads held tightly. It took both him and Austin pulling me out to get me free. I fell back and began frantically trying to brush the awful white thread from my body as the others chuckled.

"Come on, man, what's a little cobweb going to do to you?" said Austin, pulling a tuft of it from my hair. I opened my mouth to answer, but when I started to speak, all I heard was a sort of screeching hiss. My eyes fell to the spider web tunnel, and I just barely caught sight of dozens of glowing green globules in the mottled dark.

"Spiders!" I cried, and the sound of the swarm filled our ears. "Fall back!"

We stumbled back, slipped between two of the wooden supports into a tiny alcove. Katy jammed some wooden planks between the supports to try to deter the spiders from entering. Just in time she did, too, for as she stepped back, a thud sounded against other side of it. At least ten spiders the size of large dogs began to try to force their bodies through the narrow opening.

"What are these things?" shouted James over the din. "They're not like any spider I've seen before!"

He was right. These were a dark green color and had shining, green eyes, not at all like the black-bodied, red-eyed, larger variety to which we had grown accustomed. Their fangs were longer, their bristles less pronounced. On their abdomens was a peculiar mark, and they emanated an acrid scent. I could almost feel the poison in their mouths.

I dropped my pickaxe and slid a sword from its sheath, jamming the end of the blade directly into the face of one of the invading bugs. It screeched and scrambled back, disappearing behind the other spiders, who took its place.

"They may not be the same spiders we know, but they will still die just like them!" I said and stuck again through the narrow opening. Looking back over my shoulder, I saw Austin heft an axe, James pull a similar blade from his pack, and Katie leaning into her bow to string it. That's my team; that's my team. I struck again then ducked to the side as Austin's axe replaced me, a spray of green slime accompanying its strikes. Above his head, two arrows thudded into the throng, and James ducked low to slash at the legs and abdomens under the brace.

Thanks to their girth not allowing entry to our alcove, we were able to make quick work of this wave.

"Now, before more of them come out of those webs, let's take care of them," Katy said, already getting her flint and steel out to set them ablaze. We unwedged the plank and hurried back to that awful tunnel. With weapons readied, we watched Katy light the webs. They went up like flash powder, nearly instantly, accompanied by the screeches of what could only have been more of the hellish creatures. The whole tunnel was illuminated brightly for a moment, and then everything went dark. No more sound issued from the tunnel.

A simultaneous sigh of relief echoed in the now-silent stone hall. I stuck a torch into a cranny in the wall to make sure we could see, and something caught my eye. About fifteen steps into the tunnel, a wooden box with metal bands holding it together glittered.

"And our first discovery!" I said, striding toward it. I slid the sword back into its sheath and bent down to look at the box. I kicked it open.

Inside the box, there were five heat-formed gold ingots, a small sachet of seeds, a roll of string, and a handful of absolutely stunning diamonds.

Austin clapped his hands once. "Jackpot, boys and girls." We loaded up the spoils, and pressed onward. Navigating the tunnels was something interesting, but we continued forward, making sure to mark the stone so we could get back without being helplessly lost.

The tunnel led through dark, damp, open caves, the track rolling across a bridge high above the depths of ravines, and every now and again, a lone skeleton would lob an arrow our way, or a zombie would stumble off the edge of the path and fall to its doom.

All in all, we found four more crates during our exploration, and, laden with the goods we found, we emerged from the hole just as the sun was falling below the horizon. Back in the house, we spread out our haul.

Diamond, gold and iron ingots, seeds, cocoa beans, leather tunics and boots . . . The most mysterious items were the three black discs, each with a small hole in the center and a single spiral leading to the outside edge. There was a label in the center, paper cut into a circle and glued on, which had a picture of a strange device drawn on it.

"What do you think these are?" said Mary, inspecting one of them closely. "They can't just be decorations, can they?" She studied the label in the center. It seemed to have writing on it, though it was no writing that any of us could read. The device depicted seemed to be a box with a circle on top, ostensibly a place to put the disc. Small dots with tails seemed to emanate from the box. "Mysterious . . ."

The next morning we worked on building an irrigated farm. Mary's admonition was that if we could go play in a ruin for an entire day and get nice things, then we could help her build the thing that would allow us to continue going on adventures because we have eaten well. It made sense. The whole day, we dug trenches, carried buckets of water, tilled the ground, and planted seeds. The sachet of seeds we got from the tunnels was also planted, though we were not exactly sure what they would become. Finally, just as Mary finished fertilizing the soil with a huge pile of bonemeal, we went inside.

Anne had gone inside an hour or so before us, and I expected she was just tired or something. When we came back inside, however, there was sawdust all over the first floor's stone flooring, and Anne sat on top of a contraption, looking proud of herself.

"I was thinking about this thing," she said, holding up one of the discs. "The diagram on the label was a huge clue as to what it was. I figured, if I could vaguely copy the shape of the apparatus on the label, then maybe I could make this thing do what it was supposed to do."

Austin laughed, clapped her on the shoulder. "That's my Anne! So, did you figure it out?"

She knocked on the contraption. It was a wooden box, with a rotating table on the top of it, over which hung a sort of thin arm, tipped with a diamond, its point meticulously oriented downward. She wound a crank on the side and slid open a panel on the front of it, revealing the rotation mechanism and what appeared to be a very wide cone attached to a tube.

"You guys are not going to believe this." She grinned ear-to-ear, and dropped the disc onto the rotating table. Carefully, she positioned the arm over the disc and then let it down so that the point of the jewel scratched along its surface.

Nothing happened for a bit, but just as the feeling that we'd been had started to set in, a sound issued from the cone. It was . . . music?

Yes, it was! Music, a soft melody that played over a sort of low resonation, and little percussions keeping time! How on earth . . . ?

"These things, these discs," she said, holding up two more of them, "they are like written-down sound! And this device on the labels can read the sounds to us. How intense is that?"

We had a party that night, Katy baking up cakes and pies as Austin and Anne prepared a feast. I set up the great table, draping a deep red-dyed wool cloth over it. James and Mary bustled here and there making sure that everything was safe and locked up because we were not going to have any disturbances in our party tonight. We had a machine that played music! Tons of great food! Good company!

"We've made some great discoveries these last few days," Austin was saying. "Proof of previous inhabitants, an extensive system of caves, and today, Anne has found us the technology to listen to sounds that were recorded long in the past. This party, my friends, is because we're the best!" he said with a fist pump, and we all cheered at this. Drinking! Eating! Dancing! Only the best for the explorers, inventors, and heroes!

The party went well into the night, and when I awoke the next day, the sun had already climbed high into the sky. We had breakfast hastily because everyone was excited to go back into the mines, Anne and Mary included this time. Everyone gathered their gear, and we skipped into the mine shaft, heading for the entrance to the Old Tunnels, as we had taken to calling them.

The danger of spiders was of course still there, as was the occasional other monster, but for the most part, we worked as a well-oiled machine and navigated several of the tunnels, mapping out how they turned and twisted while gathering the items from the boxes that we found.

It was only when the tunnel that we were in ran directly into a huge cavern deeper than any of us had ever seen before that we stopped for pause. The sheer heat in this ravine was staggering, and it smelled like fire and rot. The reason was clear as to why: through the bottom of this ravine flowed a river, not of water, but of molten stone. We must be getting very deep for there to be actual live lava actively flowing at a reasonable pace. That must be how this ravine had formed, magma flowing over it and melting the stone over which it passed, deepening the crevice and bringing along more and more stone.

Austin's eyes lit up. "There!" he pointed to the edge of the lava flow. "That's the stone I was telling you about! Smooth, black stone formed from the very bowels of the earth! If we can get down there and get some of that, we'd never find anything stronger to build with!"

He hurriedly pounded a piton into the wall, looped his rope through it, and was just about to jump over the side to rappel down the sheer cliff face when Anne stopped him, grabbing him by the back of the belt. "What, are you stupid? You'll be incinerated."

"Yeah, if I touch it! That's the plan—don't touch the lava." He pushed himself back and over the ledge, his rope taking the slack and becoming taut in the piton. We watched as he lowered himself down, Anne pinching the bridge of her nose.

"He's a fool sometimes . . ." she muttered.

He reached the bottom after a few minutes of descent, the rest of us helping to belay him down. He unhooked his rope. "Okay, everyone, I'm good! It's hot down here, but I'm not in any danger. I'm going to try to break off some of this stuff," he said, and unslung his pickaxe. The iron head sang through the air, arcing downward to the focal point of its tip, and a dull clang-thud echoed up the cavern. Austin dropped the pickaxe and swore loudly, frantically shaking his hands back and forth.

"Yipes, this stuff is hard! My pick just broke on it," he said, sucking his teeth. "That really hurt." He sat down on a rock for a moment. "Yeah, no way we can get this stuff with just the tools we have now. We'd need something a lot harder."

James, in a flash of insight, rigged up a worktable with some wood from one of the tunnel supports and laid down a couple of the diamonds we'd found on the way here. "Think we can make a pickaxe with a diamond head? That's harder, for sure," he said, and began putting together a pickaxe but with diamonds instead of iron. He held up the finished product, a heavy-looking tool with a glittering, blue head.

We belayed it down to Austin on the rope. He untied it and hefted it in his hands. He looked up and gave a thumbs-up to us, and then heaved it over his shoulder, bringing it crashing down into the black, glassy rock.

The heavy tip bit deep into the stone, shearing it on a natural fault, and with a few more strokes, it freed a large chunk of it from the ground. Austin reached down, picked it up. "I could get used to this!" he called up, waving the stone at us. The light reflected off it in such a way that even from way up where I was, I could see it sparkle from the inside, as though a thousand tiny fires were hidden within.

He hooked himself and the bag of the black stone he'd mined back up to the rope, and we began to haul him back up the cliff face.

"The funny thing is," said Anne, as she gripped the rope in her hands, "he'd never let me tie him up any other time!" We had a good laugh, and I looked over the side to check Austin. He wasn't laughing.

"Oh, come on, it's just a bit of fun!" I called, hauling another arm's length of rope up, but he shook his head and pointed laterally to him toward a ledge in the face of the great cliff.

"I see something," he said, almost in a whisper, and he motioned us to stop pulling him up. Slowly, he grabbed onto the rough rock wall and began to move toward the ledge. As he approached, he moved slower, almost at a crawl, as though he was trying not to be seen. He grabbed the edge of the projection and pulled himself onto it, out of the range of our light sources.

We waited for a few seconds in silence and saw the rope moving as Austin moved deeper into the dark. Then, suddenly, the rope gave slack, and Austin shot out of the darkness, jumping off the edge of the little outcropping and scrambling to get away from it.

"Pull me up pull me up PULL ME UP!" he shouted, just as a low static sound, like a growl from a creature who didn't know how to make a sound we would understand, echoed through the cave complex, seeming to come from all directions at once. It was like I could feel it in my head, not just hear it. In the dark, I caught a glimpse of burning violet.

"Get him up!" We hauled with all our might, bringing Austin up, bustling him over onto the edge, and as he unhooked himself from the rope, there was a sound like quickly dragging a stick over a rough patch of gravel. Something appeared behind him.

The creature was enormously tall—at least three meters in height—and had long, spindly limbs that bent too many times in too many directions all at once. Its entire body was a sheer, dull black, with what looked like tiny sparks of the same deep violet I could see emanating from it. Its torso was long and skinny, almost emaciated, and it had no neck. Its head was attached directly to the body, a huge, bulbous skull that unhinged itself and seemed to grotesquely bare a mouth with no teeth or tongue but only jagged shards of its skull where it separated. The worst of it was its eyes, blazing in a fiery deep purple that seemed to simultaneously burn like fire and seep out like blood from erratic holes in its skull that seemed to be constantly changing shape. Its limbs terminated abruptly with no hands or feet to speak of, and from its open skull issued that same horrid dragging sound we heard before.

Austin spun, his axe snatched from its harness at his hip, and he struck at the creature, putting his strength behind the blow. It bit into the thing's brittle flesh, and Austin prepared to pull the axe back, when—

Suddenly the thing wasn't there, instead standing several meters behind James. Austin's blow continued on, and when he recovered, the thing closed in on James. Not one to be slow on the reaction, James rolled to one side, sword already in-hand, and swung the blade at where the thing was only a fraction of a second ago, but it was already somewhere else, in the darkness where we could not see.

We fled. Whatever this thing was, it was not something we wanted to fight, with its disappearing and reappearing where and whenever it wanted, so we retreated backward, into the mine rail tunnel that had brought us to the cliff. The tunnel was well-lit, and as we fell back, we thought the creature would not follow us into the light. We were wrong.

That sort of drag-scratch-zip sound echoed again, and I found myself face-to-face with the thing, crouched low and looking not unlike a mutated spider. One of its limbs struck out, seized the front of my bag harness, and hefted me off the ground, hurling me to one side. I felt my body smash into the wooden support, heard the wet thud of my head connecting with it, and felt a warm trickle run down the back of my neck. I blinked hard, fighting back the dizziness, and forced myself back to my feet. As my eyes came back into focus, I saw Katy drawing a bead on the thing with a bow.

One arrow fired and buried itself in the thing's torso. This time, it didn't disappear and let the blow come harmlessly through; this time, a neon-looking purple liquid sprayed from the wound, and the thing screeched like the sound of a knife being dragged across a chalkboard.

It stumbled and then disappeared, leaving a puddle of the acrid liquid where it was. "Arrows!" Katy cried, and everyone who had brought a bow drew them out. I slumped back against the wall, blotted the back of my head momentarily with a scrap of wool, and quickly drew out my bow.

It had appeared further down the tunnel, its eyes blazing, and it began to charge toward us, as though it would bowl through us. Five arrows (mine missed, went wide, as I was not yet focused) slammed into its body, and it let out another cry. This time it appeared just in front of Mary, who, realizing her chance, dropped the bow, seized a sword, and grabbed the thing's skull with one hand, plunging the point of the blade into its open mouth with her other hand. A sort of gurgling sound issued from its mouth, and it spasmed, thrashed, and then collapsed, its body rapidly decaying and melting into a puddle of the same violet slime. In the center of the puddle, the only thing that did not dissolve was what appeared to be a glass sphere, roughly fist-sized, green on the outside but a dark color toward the center. It rolled in the slime toward Mary's feet.

Everyone waited for a moment, not yet certain what else would happen, but when the tunnel was silent for that moment, a simultaneous sigh of relief leaked from everyone's lips. Mary and Austin rushed to my side, seeing the blood still running down my back over the top of my bag.

We set up a rest camp temporarily in that tunnel, blocking off either end of it with wood and stone. Inside, we rested for a while, heating up and eating soup or meat on a makeshift furnace and lounging about on our packs. I washed my head wound in a bucket of water. Mary had picked up the glass ball and was intently studying it, holding it up to the light, then weighing it in each hand, then tapping on it with her knuckles.

"I've got nothing," she said and tossed it to James. He reached out to catch it, but it slipped from his fingers, and pinged against the ground. Suddenly Mary, who was nearly eight meters away from James, slammed into his body at a high speed. The two of them tumbled on the dusty ground, coming to rest tangled up in a coil of rope.

Mary swore. James swore more.

"What was that about?" said James, brushing himself off as the two of them stood up. Mary was just as confused.

"That's what I want to know! Suddenly I was just flying at you, when you dropped . . . the . . ." The realization hit them both at the same time, and they both scrambled to look for the ball. It was there, just where James had let it drop, in thousands of tiny pieces.

Mary swore again. James swore more again.

And there, suddenly, was that awful low, scratching, static sound from all directions.

"Again?" cried Mary. "Seriously?" She grabbed up a weapon, knocking over the slightly red bucket of water I had been using. It flowed over the floor, making a puddle, just as that sort of warp-sound could be heard, and another of those terrible gangly black things appeared in our sanctuary.

Its leg stepped into the puddle, however, and it recoiled back, the appendage smoking and dripping green, as though it had begun to decay like the other had when it had been killed. Anne took the hint, grabbed another bucket, and flung its contents at the black thing. The water splashed over its frame, and the thing's body deteriorated before our eyes. James and Austin struck while it was busy lamenting, and it sank again to the ground, decaying like the other one, leaving a glass ball just like before.

We decided to get back out of there. This place was not the safest of places, and with me injured and the possibility at any moment of another one of those appearing paired with the fact that we no longer had any more water, it was the wisest decision we could make to go back up to the Green.

Following the marks we had left on the stone walls, we headed back until we got to a fork in the path, where a very certain piece of stone seemed to be conspicuously missing. On the ground by the hole in the stone wall, a crumbled chunk of stone—one with the marking we had left still partially visible in the pieces—lay strewn about. There was a hint of violet film on the stone, both in the wall and on the floor.

"Those things messing up our markings . . ." Anne mumbled. "Does anyone remember which way it was?"

We did not. The consensus was to make a new mark and travel in one direction for a while. If we did not find any of our marks, we'd turn around and go back the other way. Down the left passage we went, more and more paranoid about those terrible creatures. The further we went, though, the less it looked like we were going the right direction, until a sudden slope going upward spit us out on the beach, a kilometer or so south of the housing complex.

This time, Austin swore, and everyone echoed it.

At the very least, we were out of the Underground. As far as I knew, those things would not follow us up into the light, so we were at least marginally safe. The sun was on its way down, but we would have plenty of time to get back to the house if we kept up a good pace. My head wound was already getting better and had mostly closed up after we rested and ate, so I felt alright enough to push for home.

This far south of the complex, the jungle began to thin out and transition into a sort of fertile plain, covered in grass and flowers. It was huge and open, and the plan was one day to build a bigger, more inclusive, better complex there so that we'd have everything we needed in one building. For now, though, all we used it for was scouting livestock that showed up, bringing them back to the farm on leads.

The trek back to the house didn't take terribly long, though we stopped once or twice for rest, food, and collecting wood and apples. By the time we got back to the house, the sky had begun to glow that sort of orange-purple mix it turns when you know the monsters are gearing up to come out, and all of us had full bags of stuff to sort out and get into proper places. As we opened the door to go inside, an arrow thudded into the wall right next to me. Good timing.

The topic of the giant, black monster-things needed to be breached, but nobody wanted to do it. Katy openly avoided it, instead setting off to cook up some meats and soups for the evening. Austin was obviously thinking about it, but not saying anything. Mary tried to bring it up a few times, but it seemed like that subject would just have to wait until later.

She took out the glass ball, and set it on the table carefully. "At least," she said, "let's talk about this thing."

The information we could gather on it was only rudimentary: that they seemed to be terribly fragile, that they seemed to make some kind of high-speed acceleration happen when they broke, and that they came out of killed black monster-things. That brought up the subject of how the things were killed, namely best by arrows from far away or by water. Melee weapons did not work well because it would teleport away to somewhere else as soon as it got hit, which finally breached the whole subject! There we go, I thought.

"So, what on earth are those things?" Mary asked, sticking a paring knife into the table and pulling it back out idly. "They showed up when Austin went into that shadow. What was over there, man?"

Austin shrugged. "I saw a box, but it was black like the lava stone and had green fittings. When I went to open it, that thing appeared, startled me. I had to get away from it, so I ran, and that's where you guys come back in." He nodded. "I mean, I could not take that thing alone, so . . ."

"Of course, of course," said Anne. "But it appeared when you touched the box?"

"Yeah, it sort of warped right in front of me just when I put my hand on it."

"Then," said James, "the source of our problems is that box. We go find it, see what it is, see if we can't get rid of it and the black things." He held up a pouch full of gunpowder.

It was the best idea we had at the time.

Navigating back to the ledge took no time at all, and we were prepared this time. No loot bags, no extra stuff. I strapped an axe and a sword to my belt, swung a bow over my shoulder, and then slung two big buckets of water over the other shoulder. The piton Austin had used before was still there, and we added five more to lower ourselves down on pulleys. All six of us stood on the shadowed outcropping of stone on which Austin first met the creature.

Anne lit a torch, the sulphurous flash casting a grossly distended shadow of our forms across the ground. She pounded the butt of the torch into a crack in the wall, and as my eyes adjusted to the light, I saw the black box.

I cannot describe how captivating this box was. Its smooth obsidian surface incandesced with a scintillating glow, first green and then red and then blue from another angle. The lock on the front was a smooth emerald stone that, when I gazed into it, felt like it was trying to draw my very breath from my chest. I just had to open it, just had to get the treasure I absolutely knew was inside.

I was not the only one who felt this urge, it seemed, as my hand met with Mary's and Austin's as I reached for the emerald latch. Together, the three of us slowly opened the top of the box while Katy, Anne, and James made sure that nothing came from the shadows.

The inside of the box seemed to be deeper than it should have been and was impossibly black. Inside the box, there were four bundles of a yellow powder that was almost hot to the touch and gave off significant light when exposed to the air. I wondered briefly who put them there, but my thoughts were mostly on the box. I had to focus.

Why had the box called those creatures? Why didn't it call them this time? Where were they, and where did they come from? What did they want? I didn't have a lot of time to consider these things, as when Austin shut the top of the box, that dreadful low, dull, long sound that grew in intensity and signaled the oncoming of the creatures came from all sides, just like before.

"Stand your ground!" We made a circle, our backs together, and waited for the first one, all bows drawn and ready.

They came in waves, two at a time, for what seemed like forever, but our plan was phenomenally successful. When the first one appeared, we would dump some water at our feet. We would shoot it, so that it would warp—most likely nearest us—and be affected by its aversion to water. As it would start expressing its negative opinion of the stuff, we would douse it with more water and then let it do its thing. Then we'd simply collect all glass spheres at the end.

The plan went off without a hitch, no major errors or mistakes. Nobody was seriously injured, and in all, we came out with almost a dozen of those glass balls.

We finished the excursion by taking a pickaxe to the box, breaking it from the stone on which it had been bonded, and bringing it back up to the surface with us.

"And so ends the story of the horrible black monster-things," said Anne, back in the house, as the six of us sat, eating grilled fish and baked potatoes and pumpkin pies. "I don't think they will be coming around any longer to make small talk," she added, and everyone laughed. It seemed honestly like we were safe, but I had no idea what we had just caused. That night, I slept peacefully, thinking we were once again safe from those terrible warping things.

I woke up first the next morning. It was my day to get milk from the cows, so I grabbed a stack of buckets and opened the front door. Everything was silent, as it should be, but something in the early morning silhouettes was wrong. I could see almost as if there had been a fence built out of what looked like solid iron blocks, T-shapes going along in a row sticking out of the ground some twenty meters outside of the house line.

"What on earth . . ." I approached the closest one, a huge, heavy T-shape standing on the ground, its root buried in the soil. Strange marks all over its surface belayed that these were somehow melded or bonded together, but a single tap of my knuckles proved them to be solid iron.

Definitely not here yesterday, and definitely not put up by us. I turned, bolted back into the house, and roused everyone from their sleep.

"Dude, what the—?" James said, rolling out of his bed. "It's like the crack of dawn. What on earth would you—"

"No, listen, everyone, look outside. Just look," I said, swinging the door open. Sure enough, there they were, silent, iron monoliths in the morning sun. It was only then, when the sun had finally come up over the horizon fully, did I see the faint, violet shine on them, like someone had spilled some dye on the stone and tried to wipe it away in spots.

Everyone knew exactly what that meant. "Bring them down," said Katy, calmly and lowly. Pickaxes out, the monoliths all came down in less than an hour, the iron blocks all buried by the beach. None of that around my house, thank you.

The next morning, they were there again, closer this time. Again, we tore them down, and again, we buried the blocks down by the beach next to the first set of blocks. This was a great deal of iron, but where was it coming from?

On the third morning, a sort of hushed panic buzzed through us. These things kept getting closer every night! And the iron from the day before was never even taken from the beach! Where was this coming from, who was putting it there, and could those things really come above ground? We needed answers! We needed a plan!

We'd torn them down yet again, but before we took the pieces to the beach, Austin stopped us. "No, bring it inside. Let's make us some armor and weapons from this stuff and stake out the top of the house tonight. We figure out just how these things are getting here, and we stop the things that are doing it. We all know it's those creatures, but if we can fight them on our terms, then we'll have no problems at all. Let's get to work."

All six of us worked at anvils and work tables until noon settled over us, except again for Anne, who, seemingly having noticed something about her anvil, had scurried off to the storage room. She came back a few minutes later with the stack of books we'd found in boxes in the mines and plopped them down on the floor.

We didn't ask because we knew she would explain anyway. "See how these anvils have this sort of v-shape here? And how there's always this little ledge at the bottom of the v? That's to put books here, I bet," she said, opening the one on top and settling it onto the little stand portion of the iron tool. As soon as the book found its place, the pages suddenly fluttered, turning to a page full of diagrams and symbols and glyphs none of us could read. There was one glyph that we could all understand, though: it showed a man hitting a sword with a hammer and the sword glowing.

Taking up a newly-forged sword, she laid it on the anvil, picking up a hammer. It seemed to ring in her hand, and when she struck the sword with the hammer, the most extraordinary thing happened. The book exploded, all the glyphs and symbols on the pages flying off the paper and lining the sword's edge, burning into the metal. It all happened rather quickly and was over just as soon as it started, but the sword that lay on the anvil now gleamed like silver. She picked it up, and her eyes widened then narrowed into a sly smile.

"Ladies and gentlemen," she said, "we've got a magic sword."

We all fell upon the books, sorting them into the tools indicated by the glyphs on the pages. These were for armor, and these were for swords, and these were for bows. All in all, we had ten books.

We deemed Anne to be our new designated enchantress, and by the end of the hour, the stash of newly-magical tools we had included three swords, a bow, two helmets, a breastplate, and three pairs of boots. Near as we could tell, we were properly magicked-out, and for the rest of the day, we laid out battle plans for when the black things came. Buckets of water lined the roof of the house, and we built parapets where we could hide inside and shoot from. Austin primed our music box so we'd fight in good spirits, and for good measure, he reinforced the front doorway of the house with the black stone he'd managed to get from the mine.

The time came, and at sundown, as a huge bank of clouds rolled in over the house, I stowed myself in a parapet on top of the house and waited. Four on top of the house, two inside the house at the windows, we waited. Sure enough, at around midnight, we heard the shuffling sound of creatures dragging and walking and scrambling up toward our house. Nearly two dozen of the black things appeared from the tree line.

That many? We didn't stand a chance.

All of them carried a single cube of iron with them, and they began to put them together, joining them together with what must have been their acrid body-fluid (which, I suppose, would explain the violet shimmer) into those t-shapes. We waited. Austin and James downstairs would give the signal, and dash out with swords drawn. Each had a magic sword, a pair of magic boots, and a helmet. Austin wore the breastplate. When they dashed out, we would give cover with arrows and water, until there was a good opportunity to jump down and begin attacking with water.

A few of them were carrying something we had not yet seen in the t-shaped idols, though— pumpkins. Pumpkins? I watched as one of them placed a pumpkin on top of one of the t-shapes.

The thing stepped back, and it took a second or two before I noticed that the pumpkin was changing shape, that the whole iron structure was twisting and shaping into a massive, almost three-meters-tall figure with hulking arms and chest covered with green, glowing veins.

"Stop the pumpkins!" I heard James yell. They had seen it too—good.

"Arrows!" I cried, and the four of us on the roof let arrows fly toward the ones with the pumpkins. From that far away, they could not see the attack coming, and the sharpened points bit into the brittle, black flesh of four of the creatures that held the yellow squashes. The screeching that echoed through the night indicated that the battle had begun.

Austin and James burst from the doors, and they charged for the nearest creatures, a bracer of bottles of water strapped across each of their chests. Austin's sword sang, bit into the flesh of one of the black things. Instead of it instantly teleporting, however, it was lifted off the ground and flung far back toward the trees. As soon as it hit the ground, it skidded for a half-second and then disappeared. I could almost feel Austin's laugh resonate. He liked his new sword. James, for his part, severed one of the thing's limbs in one clean snick, the thing shrieking and flailing about for a second before disappearing, and reappearing far back behind the iron t-shapes.

A thunderclap suddenly resounded high above us. Lightning flashed across the sky, and a resounding crash of lightning struck down on one of the iron totems, the smell of ozone filling the air.

In that moment, the iron monster finally took its shape. It reared back, opened its mouth, and bellowed as the rain began to fall. It started lightly at first, but quickly graduated to coming down in sheets, a heavy, solid cloudburst.

The sudden stillness on the field of battle was eerie, but worse was the curdling cry that followed as so many of the twisted, angular monsters suddenly were being consumed by the water from the sky. Almost like a hive-mind decision, every single one of them disappeared at the same time.

What did not disappear was the now fully-formed iron giant lumbering toward Austin and James. I drew back my bow, felt the tingle of magic setting into the arrow, and let it fly, speeding straight at the giant. It struck the behemoth in the side of its head, its wicked, curved nose twitching at the impact. The arrow shattered into splinters, but it did manage to knock the giant back a few steps, keeping it from being in range to presumably pick Austin up and rend him in half.

We were not prepared for this.

James shouted to us, "Gonna need backup down here!" The four of us immediately jumped down from the roof, discarding the bows and drawing out more conventionally closer-range weapons. Six of us, versus one terrifying beast made of iron? Sure, no problem at all. I hoped.

Mary had the third magic sword, and as she ran toward the monster, she let the tip of it drag lightly on the ground, leaving a line of fire behind her. She jumped, and brought the sword down onto the shoulder of the golem, its magic blade finding purchase and biting into the metal. At the same time, Austin's sword slammed into its legs, sweeping it to one side enough for James's sword to attack the melted gash that Mary's sword had created. In the meantime, Katy's axe came spinning from the side and slammed into the thing's back. It roared again, the sudden onslaught apparently damaging its near-impenetrable frame, and one of its great arms seized James around the waist, flinging him high into the air.

He hit the ground with a wet thud and coughed, spitting up a gout of blood. I threw down a loop of stout rope at the thing's feet, and as it stepped forward into it, I yanked on the rope, trying to force its two legs together and throw it off balance. The rope snapped like a spider web, and it spun, its fist crashing into my chest and tossing me aside like a ragdoll. Mary, too, tried to attack it again, her sword burning red with fire even in the heavy rain, but the great fist of the monster sent her tumbling back at the house, where she struck the black stone-rimmed front door, her flaming sword carving a nick into it. The monster followed after her, but suddenly she wasn't there. In the door frame, a dark, blackish fog billowed, obscuring Mary from view. She started to yell something, but then her voice suddenly lowered and stuttered, as though she was moving away from us at a high speed. The golem fumbled into the fog after her and disappeared as well.

A gust of wind in the storm cleared some of the fog just enough to show that the doorway into our house was no longer that at all—the scenery through the black archway was that of some hell-blasted landscape, burning stone and sulphurous air. I caught a glimpse of Mary scrambling to her feet, turning with her sword again in hand, before the fog obscured the portal again.

The others looked at me. I didn't have time to ask what they wanted to do. I took a deep breath, nodded, and we all dashed for the black door.

# Hell and Back

The black stone shimmered with some kind of energy, and a thick grey-purple fog drifted out of the doorway it framed, filling the air with the scent of brimstone and pouring heat into the night air.

Everything was silent, save for a sort of warbling, phasing sound that faded in and out, coming from the doorway and the steady fall of rain. We all stood in shock, staring at the doorway, where the giant monster made of iron and our friend Mary had disappeared, weapons in hand and drenched to the bone.

"After them?" suggested James, but by that time I was already running. Everyone else took the hint, and all at once, we dove through the doorway.

Being transported through a dimensional rift is something strange. It feels like it takes several minutes, but that may be only because your perception of time might be sped up to great lengths, causing you to be achingly aware of everything that happens. Your insides feel like they are being mixed with a ladle, and your eyes seem to malfunction, inverting colors one second before switching to all-red, to all-green, to pastels, to neon. The entire process takes three seconds at the most, but they are the longest three seconds of your life.

I stumbled out of the fog, my feet only barely remembering how to hold my body up in time, into a blasted landscape, where soft, crunchy-looking stone dotted with pools of fiery lava and flows of the stuff came down from a ceiling that was impossibly high. Expansive, infinite lakes of molten rock stretched to the horizon, and here and there, the stone became too loose, and bits of it crumbled off, falling into the waiting fire-lakes to be consumed. The sheer heat of the place staggered me, but I managed to find my equilibrium just in time to watch Mary dodge one of the huge golem's fists, rolling to one side and back up to her feet. I still had my axe in my hand, so I rushed forward. The others would be there in a second or two, but in a fight like this one, every second counted.

The very stone on which we stood burned, a perpetual fire I wasn't sure would ever go out, as I swung my axe at the back of the creature's knee joint with my full momentum behind the blow. It connected just as the golem had raised its other foot to step, and so its lumbering frame began to fall backward, its support taken from under it.

"Vincent!" Mary cried and reached her hand out toward me. I knew why just a second too late, as I felt the gravelly ground under me shift. The golem slammed into the ground, and the stone under it crumbled, falling into the lava. It began to scramble, just as I was, trying to regain purchase somewhere before we fell into the fiery lake. It was at that second that I saw the others appear, and Austin dashed to grab my hand and pull me back to solid ground.

The golem, too, seemed to have gotten a hold of something solid and was dragging itself back up to its feet when suddenly Anne's metal boot crashed into the side of its head, disorienting it just enough for it to lose grip, and as it slid down into the lake, its roar pierced the hot air like a needle.

All was silent for a moment. Then, Katy grabbed James and Anne by the collar and dragged them back toward the black archway through which we'd come. Not a bad idea, we all thought at once, and in seconds we were back in the Green, the rain still coming down as though we'd never been gone . . . and in reality, we'd not been for very long.

The door to the house was still an active portal, though, and we could not get inside without finding a way to somehow turn it off. Frustrated, Austin kicked the stone, knocking it loose from its makeshift setting. Immediately, and with a sound like the sucking of water through a small hole, the fog disappeared, the sounds stopped, and the door went dark.

Inside, with the door locked, ourselves upstairs, and the stairs barricaded, everyone collapsed uneasily, catching breath while we had a chance. Who knew what else would come next.

There was simply too much stuff to talk about, stuff that needed to be addressed, so we decided to put off the whole thing until the next morning. What was left of the night, we all slept, exhausted from what had all gone down. I dreamed of giants, of black shapes, of fire. I wondered, was I the only one who dreamed so?

"We need to build in a safer place," Austin was saying the next morning, rolling out the map of the immediate area on the table. "Building in the jungle would allow for better cover, better protection for the housing complex, and we could use this place as storage. Furthermore, we could build higher up off the ground, which would offer the best kind of awareness system."

"How do we get into the house," asked James, "if it's high up in the trees?"

Austin grinned, rolled out another piece of paper on top of the map. It was a blueprint, a detailed schematic of what looked to be an elevator system. "Redstone circuitry, my friend," he said. "I have been messing with the red ore dust we've been finding in the mines, and I can confirm that when it's laid down in a line, it will transmit an impulse from one end to the other. It can do things like close doors or make Katy's music box run, so my guess is that it somehow simulates an action for whatever object it's connected to based on the object."

James stared. Austin pulled out a bag of the red dust and trailed it from where he stood to the nearby door. Taking a short stick from the pile of kindling, he lit it on fire then sprinkled some of the dust on it. The fire died out, but the end of the stick glowed like an ember. Everyone watched as Austin touched this ember to the line of dust.

The dust lit up, glowing just like the ember, and when the glow reached the door not a second later, the latch turned and the door swung open. He touched the trail again, and just like that, the door shut itself.

It was a mixture of disbelief, amazement, and confusion that wafted through the room. Austin beamed. "I bet I could engineer some intense stuff with this, if you guys give me some time to figure it out."

"Well, if it will keep us safer, then you get to work on that," James said, the rest of us agreeing. "We'll build a tree house, while you do your research. If something comes out of it, then great, but I'm going to wager you haven't got much to show us by the time we're finished."

Austin's eyes sparkled. "What's the wager?"

"If we're done with the house and you have not got anything sufficiently impressive to show us, you do my share of the planting and harvesting for three days."

"And if I do," Austin said with a grin, "then you have to wear pink leather for three days."

James grimaced. "Deal, sir." They shook hands firmly, and Austin stretched.

"Well," he said, "I'll be off to my laboratory then. See you guys in a bit."

He went off to work. I was absolutely certain Austin actually had a laboratory somewhere nearby, because that was exactly the sort of thing Austin would do. Meanwhile, the rest of us scouted a location for the tree house. It was decided that the tallest tree in the vicinity with the thickest trunk would make for the best support.

Using the vines that crept up the trunks, I climbed up some twenty meters from the ground, and began nailing planks down to make a platform on which to stand. From there, the rest of my group climbed up the ladders they placed on the trunk, and we began working, expanding my platform outwards and upwards. By the time the night came, we had a sizable floor plan for three floors, a skeleton plot of where the walls and stairs would go, and the first floor reinforced and sturdy.

Austin did not show up for dinner that evening or for bed either. The next morning, we found the pantry had been raided, and several loaves of bread and pots of soup had been taken, replaced by a scrawled note that read, "Better start dyeing that leather." James grimaced.

This went on for two more nights, and at around noon of the fourth day, when we finally climbed down from the tree house that was fully finished, a wood-paneled interior with solid stone outer, accessible from a large door in the floor, we found that there was a large square of planks in the jungle floor directly below our house with a lever attached to a stone next to it. Austin lounged lazily on the stone, drinking a huge bowl of fresh milk, a box conspicuously placed next to him.

"Ladies and gentlemen," he began, and stood in the center of the square. He laid his hand on the lever. "Behold!"

He threw the lever, and a sort of whirring sound emitted from beneath his feet. Suddenly, the planks he was standing on were pushed up off the ground, and as we stood and watched, a mechanism under the planks became visible. It was a mess of red dust and metal, but its workings were plain to see: Austin had built a piston system and used it to propel the platform up to exactly the right height to be let in through the door in the floor. After a second or two, the device retracted back into the ground, Austin standing triumphantly on it still.

"And this," he said, hopping off the platform and opening the box, "is for you, James. My good sir."

Katy pulled a batch of cookies out of the furnace, and turned to place them on the table in the center of the dining room. James grumbled his thanks.

"What's wrong, dear?" asked Katy, in a voice that dripped with patronizing sarcasm.

"These pants are chafing me," he said, and scratched at the waistband of his pink leather pants.

I slid my chair back from the table. "Basically," I said, "we now know that the old stories about this place are at least partially true, that there is a 'Nether' that is reached through an archway of black stone and that it does burn and is made primarily of fire. Here's what I think. We should mount an exploration into it, see if there's anything in that land that we could use. See if perhaps there is anything that lives there, see if we can't find some allies. Find out more about our world."

Mary chuckled. "For science, is it?"

"For science."

"What of the mine tunnels? We have not yet finished mapping those out." Anne took a cookie, ate it in one bite.

"Three teams," I began. "One team explores the mines. Map them, find out the scope of their extent. If you run into something dangerous, do not confront it, and just run away. Blockade it or something and mark it on the map. One team keeps up the farm and Green operations, researching and engineering using the technology Anne and Austin have found for us. One team heads into the Nether and explores there for a couple days. At the appointed time, all parties regroup back at home, and we share findings. If any one party does not return, the other two parties become the search and rescue party for the third."

Anne chuckled. "I'm all for this plan, providing I can be in the engineering group. I'm not too terribly fond of having to fight more stuff."

James volunteered to be in the mines group, and Katy followed suit. Austin answered without a second's hesitation: "Research team." That left Mary and myself on the Nether Exploration Squad, a task about which Mary seemed quite excited. This plan was officially in effect.

Our official motto for this plan was decided, and with a good laugh, everyone put their hands in the center, and took a deep breath.

"For science!"

Mary and I packed our gear up as concisely as we could. A couple pickaxes, a couple shovels, some tools for a makeshift work table should we need one, one of the magic swords and the magic bow, lots and lots of rope, and at least four days' worth of rations. We also had some of the black stone and a firestarter, just in case we got lost and needed out of that place quickly. The other teams had their own preparations done, and so we gathered by the elevator platform.

"Well, everyone," said Mary. "Let's get to work!"

She and I headed toward a small stone shack we'd erected to house the entrance to the Nether. The portal inside glowed and spewed black and purple fog. The sound of fire crackling could be heard through the dull whooshing and dragging ambience that the portal generated. Mary looked at me, and I nodded. In we went.

This was the third time we'd been through the portal, but it still felt disorienting and awkward and sickening all at once. I wondered if we would ever become accustomed to that feeling, the feeling of being disassembled in one world and reassembled in another. The thought briefly crossed my mind that the possibility we would be incorrectly reconstructed in this fire land existed, but I decided not to think too hard on it.

We set to work on the other side, building a similar shanty around the portal there as a sort of safety hole in which to hide should we encounter something unpleasant. Once we'd built up a little shelter there, we began.

We picked a direction and began to travel. The ground was the same red, crumbly stone that smelled of oil, and here and there, little fires on the ground simply burned with no indication of stopping. High up above, there seemed to be clusters of some kind of brightly-shining stone precariously hanging from the crumbly red stone. Here and there, buried in the erratic walls of the place, I noticed slivers of a white, marble or quartz-like substance. Pickaxes made short work of the surrounding stone, and we found that the quartz-like ore was actually rather pretty to look at and could be made into something nice perhaps. We took a rest by a low overhang, on which grew some of that brightly glowing rock. It broke into a sort of spongy powder very easily. What I did not see, however, was any sign of life.

Until we turned around a corner of the giant cavern, and saw the great, flat plain that terminated on a sheer cliff down below us, in the center of which stood what appeared to be a castle or fortress of some sort, surrounded by thick walls some four meters high. The whole plain was dotted with figures, aimlessly shambling here and there. From here, they looked like . . . pigs?

Mary shook her head. "No, no way. Not even going to go that direction. We're turning around and going somewhere else."

I hesitated.

"Don't even think about it, Vincent; don't you even consider it. Look at how many of them there are!"

I took a deep breath.

"I'm telling you right now," she insisted, "we're going to avoid this place here and just go on exploring somewhere else. Opposite direction, let's about-face right now."

A sort of whine, like the kind you'd hear a cat wail when they are bored or hungry—but sped up in frequency—shattered my decision-making train of thought, and I looked up just in time to see something massive floating above us in the air, quite far away but still very big. It looked not unlike a bloated, white squid with tentacles dangling below it, swaying to and fro as it floated. Its eyes were a black and deep red and seemed to drip what might have been blood down its face, which covered the entire front of its bulbous body. Its mouth was rounded, and it did not seem to have a jaw to speak of, instead using musculature around its mouth to open and close its razor-sharp-looking teeth. It seemed to float in the air like I would float in water, and it had its terrible eyes locked on us.

It made that same sound again, opened its mouth, and spit a fireball. The projectile hurled toward us at an alarming speed, and when I grabbed Mary and dragged her violently to one side, she started to swear until the blazing sphere slammed into the stone where we were only moments before. The ground positively dissolved in the fire, and what ground was not destroyed caught ablaze immediately. Back up to our feet, I pushed Mary one way and darted the other.

"Get cover!" I yelled, and dashed to escape another oncoming blast. Mary ducked behind a jutting of rock, pulled out her bow, and nocked an arrow. I hazarded a glance back toward the plain with the stronghold in it and saw all the figures still shuffling like nothing was going on.

Mary held up her hand to signal me, and I nodded. "I'll draw its attention!" I affirmed and ran back toward the thing, zig-zagging as I did so. The pale squid-thing pelted the ground with explosive balls of fire, singeing my heels as I dashed here and there. It was long enough of a distraction, however, for Mary to aim and fire, the arrow gaining speed and force like it never could have without magic.

The arrow buried itself fletching-deep into the side of the creature. "Yes!" I intoned, watching the thing quiver for a moment . . . but it did not fall. It instead opened its mouth again and launched yet more fire at me. "Again! More of that!" I called, and continued trying to avoid the fire. All around me, patches of intense flame burned, blocking my path here and there, so I had to continue until I was almost directly under it.

It let loose a hail of fire, one after the other, trying to pin me into one spot and then torch me to death, but just at that moment . . . !

Thud, thud, thud! Three more arrows in succession slammed into the thing, sending it reeling back in the air, screeching. It leveled with me and spit one last fireball, but I drew out my sword and slammed it back with the flat of the blade, sending it hurling directly into the thing's face. The ball exploded, and with a great wail, the thing's semi-gelatinous body began to deteriorate as it fell out of the air, making a wet, disgusting splat as its body connected with the rock.

Its body gradually seeped into the cracks in the stone, and after a few seconds, nothing was left but a single sparkling gem, shaped like a teardrop and encasing what appeared to be some kind of liquid. Warily, I picked it up, and found it was cool to the touch.

We rested, in a cave we hurriedly dug out of one of the nearby walls. Water, food, and rest for about an hour, and the both of us felt good enough to begin travelling again.

"So, while we were fighting this thing, it screeched and whined pretty loudly. Even so, it seemed like those things down there didn't notice or didn't care. Do you think they can hear?" I asked.

Mary shrugged, stretched a bit, and checked how many arrows she had left. "I still don't think it's a good idea to go that way."

I grabbed a chunk of loose rock, went to the edge of the low cliff, and hurled it down at the plain. It struck the ground right next to one of the figures, breaking into little pieces. The thing did nothing.

"But there's that castle there! Aren't you even curious what's inside?"

"Just as curious as you," she said, clicking her tongue, "only slightly more careful."

"Let's go at least down to the same level as those things, see if they see us. If they do, we can run away."

"Vincent, so help me, if we get killed for this . . ."

We found a rough path down the cliffside, and in a few minutes, we stood on the flat plain on which was the dark brick-built keep. Some thirty meters ahead, one of the things shuffled about aimlessly. We could see them more clearly now; they stood as tall as we did but had the heads of pigs. They all carried a golden sword in hand and made curt, snorting noises as they walked about. The most unsettling factor, however, was that their flesh, all over their bodies was decayed and gangrenous, bones visible through obvious rotted holes in their skin surrounded by green and grey tissue just waiting to slough off their bodies. And yet they walked.

The zombies in the Green were not nearly this bad. Sure, their faces were distorted and their skin was a deep poison-green, but they were at least not actively decaying in front of you. These things, these zombie-pig-men, were awful to behold. I took another rock and tossed it in the direction of the closest one. It hit the ground, rolled, and stopped against the thing's foot. Still, no reaction. Hesitantly, I cupped my hands over my mouth and yelled.

"Hey! Over here! You lot!" I called, ready to run away if they turned and suddenly flew toward us or something, but . . . nothing. No response, whatsoever. It was as if they simply didn't process the world around them at all. Slowly, we approached the open plain.

The further we walked toward the decaying man-pig, the more uncomfortable Mary became, and the more the smell of decay began to soak the air we breathed. We were not ten paces away from one of them now, and still there was no response from the creatures. I took a breath, shallowly because of the smell, and walked past the pigman purposefully.

Through this huge plain filled with what must have been scores of these things, Mary and I walked as though they were merely interesting and smelly garden gnomes, them taking no interest or even notice of us. It was surreal to watch these creatures that looked like just the kind to want your flesh shuffle past with no indication that they knew you even existed, but without the threat of being eaten, I almost relaxed as we picked our way through the throng, coming up on the dark, bricked entrance to the stronghold.

The walls that surrounded the fort had little parapets on top of them and seemed to be erratically constructed, as a large chunk of the wall simply wasn't built. It wasn't like it was destroyed or something, either; it simply looked like whomever had been building the wall just didn't build this part. I ducked into the courtyard, which was admittedly just a barren five-meter break between the outer walls and the inner, and as Mary followed, I spotted a set of stairs running up into an opening.

There were no zombie pig-men inside the walls, and the smell was less horrid, though something still made my hair stand on end and put my teeth on edge as we walked down the long hallway that was the entrance. I could hear somewhere down the maze of turns we encountered the characteristic rattle of dry bones moving against each other.

The passage suddenly opened up, and the ground stretched out in a thin bridge that led nowhere, crumbling at the end of it into the vast sea of red-hot lava far below. I could see to the left that there was another bridge that led to a pillar of that same dark brick that seemed to sprout from the boiling ocean to this impossibly tall height, and the bridge was riddled with skeletons.

Skeletons, and . . . something else? It looked like a sort of glowing ball with a bunch of similarly glowing sticks swirling around a black cloud of smoke. Four of them seemed to rest over by the base of that pillar, seemingly not concerned about the skeletons.

Mary unslung her bow and fitted an arrow to the string. "Think we can take them?" she asked. "They don't look too tough. They look like the ones in the Green."

I nodded with a grin. "Don't know what those things are, but the skeletons—easy to predict, easier to dispatch. Let's get them," I said and began to open a passage in the wall toward the other bridge. We did this sort of tactic all the time—lure the skeletons into a narrow tunnel, then get up close before they could retreat, and take them apart summarily.

Mary let her arrow fly, and it crashed through the dome of one of the skeleton's skulls. It staggered, regained its balance, and turned its sightless, eyeless sockets toward her. She made an obscene gesture.

Somehow, they always knew where the shortest paths to you were. It's the same with the zombies and the giant spiders. That's their main weakness—their predictability. It turned toward the stronghold, slipped into the tunnel I opened in the wall, and when it came out the other end, I smashed it with my shovel before it could recognize I was there.

Four more skeletons went down the same way. We were a well-oiled machine in the skeleton-killing business. The four spinning glow-ball things finally seemed to notice that all the skeletons were disappearing, though, as I could make out a face on one of them when they started to move, gliding down the bridge to get closer to us.

"Same plan?" I said, shovel ready.

"Same—" Mary began but stopped short when all four of the burning things simultaneously lifted from the bridge, taking flight.

"More flyers?" I said, watching as one of them visibly bristled with living flame. "We've already killed one flying, fire-spitting monster, and it was ten times your size. Come and get us!" I yelled at the creatures, brandishing my shovel.

The correct thing to do would have been to run inside the hallway, taking cover from the inevitable onslaught of fire. I made the wrong choice.

All four creatures launched barrages of fireballs, which slammed into the walls, the bridge, and me. I briefly remember thinking that it was convenient that these ones did not explode on contact, but my next thoughts were consumed by something that probably sounded like, "AHH I AM LITERALLY ON FIRE." I dropped the shovel, immediately reached for the canister of water on my bag. As soon as I opened it, though, to my dismay, it evaporated in a massive puff of steam.

I was still on fire.

"Vincent!" Mary screamed, and, seeing that the water evaporated instantly, instead opened up a container of mushroom soup, dashing it over me and putting out the fire. I would have protested, but when more fire came down from the creatures, it was clear that we had made the right choice this time.

Behind a corner, we took stock of ourselves again, the metallic breathing of those creatures just outside echoing in the hallway. They didn't seem to want to come into the—

FIRE. More fire flew from the thing which most certainly just did come into the hallway after us. No time to rest, it seemed, as the two of us had to scramble to our feet and run again, down this hall and around the corner.

"Ambush?" Mary said through heavy breathing.

"That's all we've got to work with!" I coughed back and jerked my axe from its harness. Mary slid her sword out, and we pressed ourselves against the wall, waiting for it to come around the corner.

Somehow, I was suddenly on fire again, only briefly because the soup still kept my clothes damp. I swore and looked behind us. Down the hallway we'd ducked into, one of the blazing creatures skidded toward us.

"The things pincered us!" I growled and, with gritted teeth, dashed right at the creature, axe raised. I struck down at the thing's head, and the axe bit harshly into the metallic sphere, causing the thing to emit a grating sound, as if one metal were dragged against another. One of the rods that spun around its central body swung out and struck at me, but

I saw it coming and sidestepped so it just barely grazed my shoulder, leaving a scorch mark.

Mary, on the other hand, had her own battle to fight. The one that had been coming down the hall rounded the corner and shimmered with fire. Mary didn't wait for the inevitable hail of fire, though—she thrust her sword into the thing's head, ripped it free, and brought it down on top of it. The thing faltered, its fiery barrier momentarily blinking out, and Mary spun one, using the momentum of the swing to crash the edge of the sword clean through the thing's head, splitting it cleanly in two.

Instantly all the rods that spun around it fell clanging and clattering to the floor, beginning to cool down. Mary turned to help me, and as I dodged under another of the rods that swung at my head, I swung the axe upwards, connecting with the bottom of the head and casting it upward, into the ceiling. It cracked against the hard bricks, fell to the floor, and broke into pieces.

Two down, two to go. I felt a surge of adrenaline course through my veins. Where were they? I could hear their breathing, if it could really be called that, echoing down the hallways. Where? My fingers tightened on the axe.

I saw them, suddenly, as I looked down the hallway that led to the bridge. There the two of them were . . . flying away? What? Mary saw them too and looked just as puzzled as I did. I lowered my weapon, confused.

The heavy footsteps started a few seconds afterward—heavy in the sense that whatever was walking was obviously not trying to be quiet or subtle. It was a sort of hollow, clacking sound with a metallic clang every few steps, and the steps seemed to be far apart. It was far away, down in the labyrinth of tunnels somewhere, but I somehow knew it was coming for us.

I grabbed up a couple of the rods from the fallen blaze-creatures and jammed them into my bag. They might come in handy for something, I thought, and without even saying anything, Mary and I dove back into the hallways, trying to find our way back out to the plain. In the chase that had happened with the blazes and us, I'd lost my bearings, and Mary seemed to have done something similar. We dashed this way and that, turning corners and finding dead-ends, until we came around one corner and had to stop.

On the ground, in the center of the hallway, was a set of armor, inside of which the bones of its previous owner lay. Beside it, a broken sword lay scattered on the ground, and on its back was a pack much like the ones we had, full of equipment and other things.

The footsteps were still coming, and I wasn't entirely sure that this thing would not stand up and try to kill us, but Mary approached it and gasped.

"There's no head . . ." she murmured. She lightly shifted the pack with her foot, and it opened, spilling some things across the floor: some glass bottles with colored liquids inside, a handful of diamonds, a thick book, and . . .

Three black, grotesque skulls, slightly too large to be from a human. They tumbled a bit before coming to rest, their teeth chattering on the brick floor. Mary backed up and covered her mouth. Still, the footprints continued coming. I could not tell if they were getting closer or farther away, but I knew they were still there. And I did not want to be where they were. Hurriedly, I jammed the contents back into the bag, skulls and all, slung it over my shoulder, and grabbed Mary by the wrist.

"Move, we have to get out of here," I said in a low voice, and we took off down the hall. If we could find a hallway we'd been in before, maybe we could navigate back to the entrance, out of the stronghold, and back out of what was essentially hell. I was pretty ready to run away, go back to the Green, and brick up the portal to this place so we would not come back.

We turned this way, swung that way, and seemed to be running forever. When we rounded the next corner and saw the remains of that fallen explorer again, I let loose a torrent of choice words that would curl any mother's hair.

"Where are we?" Mary echoed my general thoughts with significantly less profanity. I unhooked my pickaxe and gritted my teeth.

"We're going to make a proper exit right now," I said, and the tip of the pick bit into the brick wall, breaking free chunks of the dark stone. Mary took up arms next to me, and in a minute or so, we had opened a sizable hole in the wall that led out into the empty courtyard only by sheer luck. Another minute or so, and the hole would be big enough to slip through.

The footsteps that kept coming suddenly came to a stop. I froze, as a feeling of sickness washed over my entire body. I could sense the pit of my stomach tightening up, and my hands shook a little bit. I forced myself to turn my head and look back behind us.

There, down at the intersection of this hallway and the next, stood a massive smoky-black skeleton at least two and a half meters tall, bones clattering together as its skull turned and looked in our direction. Its empty eye sockets twinkled with a red dot of light, and all at once I saw deep golden glyphs burn in its bones, as if they were all carved into each bone by hand and imbued with the same kind of magic that came from those books Anne had used on our tools only a few days before.

In a sudden pulse that centered on the thing, all the color around it began to fade and turn grey. It took one great step forward, the hallway quivering like it was water.

Mary gritted her teeth, sucked in a deep and quick breath. "Go, quick, let's move!" she growled, and I positively forced my body, protesting the whole way, to turn back to the hole and strike it one more time with the pickaxe. The bricks fell away, and with the last push of adrenaline my body could give me, I threw Mary through the hole and, just as the blackened skeleton raised its humongous sword up to strike, dove headfirst through the opening. Mary was already on her feet, and as the two of us barreled out of the courtyard and into the open plain again, I hazarded a glance upwards to make sure there was not another ghost waiting for us.

Back, back to the portal we ran, pausing only briefly to drink and recover, and when we arrived, there was no hesitating, no trepidation. We both leapt headlong through the portal and were deposited unceremoniously back in the little lean-to shack that housed the Green side. Out of there, we hurried back to the house.

It was nightfall when we came back to the Green, which surprised me because in the Nether there was no sun, no moon for estimating time that had passed. Mary collapsed onto the thick carpet in front of the fireplace, and as I unhooked my bags and the armor I wore, I could feel the fatigue settling in as well. Thank the stars for Austin's elevator system, or I don't think we'd have been able to get back up into the house.

Austin and Anne were out, doing engineering things, I supposed, and that was fine with me. I broke open some roast chicken from the pantry, pared it into some bowls of mushroom soup, and heated them over the fire. As they were heating, I dumped out all our spoils on the carpet next to Mary.

From the exploration, we had several small bags full of the quartz-like substance, a few more of the glowing yellow dust, loads of mushrooms, and the teardrop-shaped gem that came from the body of that awful jellyfish-squid-monster. From the bag on the dead explorer, though, there were diamonds, bottles of stuff I'd never seen before that bubbled or sloshed in ways I wasn't quite expecting, a handful of a strange, wilted sort of fungus, the three black skulls, a bag of sticky-feeling sand, and the thick, heavy book with a quill sandwiched in the pages.

Mary vaguely protested having taken a dead guy's stuff, but I opened the book to the first page and read aloud.

"Herein are the notes and observations of Pollus, explorer and great friend of mine. May your travels be fruitful and exciting, and may your adventures never find their end. Your friend and colleague, Augustus."

I turned the page, but from that point onward I could only decipher some pieces of the writing, due in part to its being written in alien characters, but also to its owner's atrocious handwriting. It looked like, at some points, there were paw-prints across the pages, and the ink was smudged and smeared here and there.

I flipped through until I found a passage I could read, guessing now and again about the characters I did not know.

"The legends are true. The ancient . . . great, black body, and its wings are a full . . . Ender-men alone, and the ground vibrates with a strange energy. Still, it is less oppressive than the Nether's . . . can flee from its terrible onslaught only so long before it will . . ."

Mary listened, rolled onto her stomach, and pulled the book toward her while I put a spoonful of the soup into my mouth. "These characters—I have seen them before," she said and then shuffled to her feet over toward the anvil, where James and Katy had apparently found another book in the mines and had put it on the shelf. She picked it up and flicked it open, compared it to the glyphs in the book that apparently belonged to "Pollus." They were the same kind of writing.

On that note, I seized up one of the black skulls and looked again. The glyphs carved into the bone were the same!

This writing system—was it the language of the people that were here so long ago?

Austin kicked the door open, holding a box of machine parts and, surprised, gave us a hey-dudes. "What are you guys doing back so soon?" he asked, setting the box down and scattering its contents on the floor to begin sorting them. "You have another day before you—"

I rolled one of the skulls at him. "This is only one of the things that attacked us violently in that place, and you would need to see some of them to believe them." I described to him the harrowing fights with the ghast, the blaze, and the black skeleton, not leaving out any of the details.

" . . . so when I got out of that castle, I had no intention of being there for even another second. Plain and simple, that place is dangerous. If we wanted to mount an assault on it, we'd have to have some kind of protection against fire that won't evaporate immediately and isn't mushroom soup." Austin listened intently.

"So what about this book, then?" he said, and I slid it over to him.

"It's my guess that over time the language that they used developed into the one we use now, by simplification or by permutation or whatever, and that's why there's a mix of the characters from the old magic books and the ones that we use. The only thing I can think of is that there was a mixing of cultures, but we've only had evidence of the one culture here."

Austin flicked the book's pages and stopped on a page near the back, where the page was nearly covered from top to bottom in some kind of rhythmic-looking chant or poem. I could only read a few words of it.

". . . call upon . . . of the darkness, the black lord, who . . . great and terrible, heed me, and . . . the steps for bringing forth the great dark lord of the underworld."

"Oh. Wow," I mumbled. "This man was trying to awaken some kind of terrible god." I turned the page, and there was a diagram, drawn with great attention to detail, of the items this man thought were needed for summoning this creature. The chant continued, but this time it was all written in the older script, and I could not read any of it.

The three of us were silent, letting the gravitas of the subject matter of this book sort of wash over us. This Pollus fellow was either mad or dabbling in the kind of magic we didn't want to touch.

I sorted out the items we brought back with us and put them in their appropriate boxes. The rods I picked up from that creature seemed too eager to fall into powder, so I wrapped them up in a scrap of wool fabric to keep them intact and placed in them in the box next to the glass orbs we'd collected from before.

The next morning, as Mary and I had technically finished our portions of this expedition, I went to go help Austin with his work, and

Mary set herself up to start doing "something in the kitchen," she said, with an almost sinister smile.

Austin grinned as we walked down toward the beach. Through the trees, I could see he had built a low, wide structure of earth and stone, the ceiling of it made entirely of glass. He beckoned me through a door in the side, and as I entered, I saw what this place was.

The humidity inside was the first thing I noticed. Even though the air outside was slightly chilly, in here it was almost too warm for comfort. The long building had several streams of water flowing down rows of soil—an irrigation system that seemed to be regulated by a row of buttons on the far wall. Each button was marked by the vegetable or fruit it controlled: pumpkins, carrots, potatoes . . .

"A greenhouse?" I asked, and Austin nodded.

"That's not the only good part. Watch this," he said and pushed the "carrots" button.

The water flow down the center of that pair of rows cut off, trickled to a halt, and then a series of pistons below the soil, which I could only see now that the water had stopped flowing, slowly pushed upwards through the soil, bringing the carrots up and dumping them over into the now-dry water trough. They all fell into a series of metallic funnels, which fed into a long pipe that seemed to lead back toward the buttons. Austin opened a box that was partially sunk into the ground, and inside the box were the carrots that had just been harvested from the earth there.

"And all that we have to do is plant some new seeds every time. Everything else? All completely automated, all redstone. I bet James is sitting pretty in his pink leathers now," he said with a chuckle. I marveled.

He showed me the schematics for the piston systems, and we got to work on the last few rows.

"I've been thinking about those black creatures," Austin confessed. "We have an idea where the monsters on the Green come from, and I am going to assume that the monsters in the Nether are just terrifying because it's hell. That leaves these alien black things, which seem out of place, and the black box from which I can only assume they came. Where are those from?"

I hazarded a guess. "Do you think they might be from the End?"

"Up until a few days ago," he said and laid down more of the sparkly red dust, "I'd have dismissed that idea. Now that all this stuff has happened, though . . ."

"Right? It's like all the things I assumed about this place were wrong, and that's pretty disorienting. I don't know what to think anymore."

"And what if we accidentally stumble across the End? What if we find ourselves there like we found ourselves in the Nether? If the other legends have been proven true, then there's a great dragon there as well. I'm confident in my ability to fight monsters, but a dragon?"

"Yeah . . ." I said and took a deep breath. "This place, man—what if we just built our compound so that there was no possibility of monsters getting in? Like, we'd light it up brightly, and build walls high enough to avoid unwanted arrow fire, and make it safe."

"That's actually a pretty good idea, but it would take loads of work and planning, and really high walls . . ."

"And," I said after a second of contemplation, "where would the adventure be?"

That was really the truth. No matter how dangerous something was, how close it came to killing me, how far it pushed my limits, I liked the adventure of it all. To take that all away just to be safe wasn't my style at all.

The channels were laid down, and the water sources were dug in. This greenhouse was officially fully-functional. And it was all done before noon. As Austin and I munched on some beef and bread, he suggested we went to see Anne's work. Anne holed herself up in the old house, which she had converted to her research room. As we approached, we could hear hammers and saws and music all coming from inside.

Austin knocked on the door as he pushed it open. Inside, Anne sat on the floor with a bunch of parts and scraps scattered around her. She looked up, covered in sawdust, and grinned.

"Hey you guys. Check this out," she said and held out the thing she was working on. It was a small item made of gold on the exterior with a dial on the inside.

"A clock? This tells the time of day! Amazing!" said Austin, looking at it from a bunch of different angles.

"That's just the tip of the iceberg," she said and motioned to the series of boxes behind her, dark, polished wood boxes joined by lines of that same redstone dust we were using before. "I know we have a device that can play music from these discs we have, but I thought, what if I wanted to create music myself? So I messed with the inside of the player box and figured out how to make devices that played notes that you told them to. Watch this," she said and pulled a lever attached to the one box at the end. It played a slow scale, eight notes up and then back down. The lever snapped itself back up when the last note finished.

It seemed that Austin stayed on the science tree, while Anne branched onto the culture tree. Those two make a great team, I thought to myself. Anne turned to me. "I've made a compass and a clock for everyone, so you guys can take yours now," she said and handed Austin and me the devices. "I'm working also on a few other things right now, most specifically this automated oven," she said and motioned toward a large stone and metal contraption behind her.

"You just put in the ingredients on top, and then it will mix them and knead them and bake them for you! Right now it only sort of works," she said bashfully. "I can't get it to not overcook and burn the breads."

We hung out a bit with Anne before I decided to head back and see what Mary had been up to all day. As I approached the tree house, I noticed an extra wing on one side of it that had not been there earlier today. I could smell something baking.

I rode the elevator upwards, and when I got inside, the whole house was covered in a thin layer of white flour. I heard bustling coming from the new wing, so I hesitantly peeked my head inside the doorway that had been installed in the wall. Mary was inside, setting down a freshly-baked cake on a shelf full of freshly baked cakes above and below similar shelves of cakes that lined all four walls of this room.

"Welcome to the cake shop!" Mary said cheerfully, wiping her flour-adorned face with her sleeve. "I figured, everyone needs some cake after all that's happened in the past few days. Tonight, we have cake!"

James and Katy arrived home, carrying humongous bags of loot. Coal, iron, lapis, redstone, gold—you name it, they had brought back tons. They'd also managed to find a few more of the chests down there and had come back with new music discs, some diamond, and one peculiarly-shaped set of armor that looked like it would fit some kind of animal. They'd mapped out something like a kilometer in each direction and had come back with detailed mapping of those areas.

It seemed that everyone had done exactly what we had set out to do. The mines had been relatively cleared, we hadn't seen any more of those awful black things, we came back alive from the dimension comprised primarily of fire and fear, and there were significant jumps in the development of technology to complement our magic. We were doing well.

True to her word, that night Mary had prepared nearly thirty cakes. We celebrated all our successes by eating cake until we could eat no more then sang and laughed and danced around Katy's fancy music contraptions until we grew hungry and ate more cake.

A week passed in relative harmony, the only problems arising being the occasional gathering of zombies and spiders and the like under the house, but since Austin installed the arrow traps at the base of the trunk, there wasn't much of an issue with it. We took several days to simply rest and relax. After all, we had stores and stores of food now thanks to the automated farm, so much iron and gold from the mining expeditions, and plenty of redstone to fiddle with in the laboratories. A couple days of lazing about would not hurt anyone.

I spent this time trying my best to decode the writing in the book, assisted by Mary primarily but also whomever felt like giving it a lookover. We found it was almost always a simple substitution cipher with few variations, and by the end of a few days we'd managed to decipher much of the writing inside. I flipped through the pages of the account I had just finished translating.

"This land is said to be a land that exists in four places at once. The plane of earth, where I reside, and the plane of fire, from whence issue monsters, I have seen with my own eyes. The remaining two are legends that have been spoken by my people for ages: the plane of darkness, wherein lives the Embodiment of the End, and the plane of sky, where it is said angels once lived. I know not what is said to have happened to such angels who 'once' lived in such a place, but if they still exist there, then I believe they have turned their backs on us and no longer busy themselves with matters of an earthly bent.

"And yet I seek both of these places, knowing full-well that they may just as likely not exist as they may contain the old dragons or angels of legends."

That's strange, I'd never heard of any sky world. This was news to me. And, "my people," he said . . . were his people perhaps the people who had become the monsters we fought? Or was he, too, from a land very different from here?

Lazily, I leaned back on a box, and it shifted, bumping into the wall behind it. I heard a dull clink from inside, and, opening the box to check what had moved, I looked inside. It turns out it was the chest that held the glass balls from those black creatures and the rods from the blaze-monsters. Over the few days since we'd come back, it seemed the rods had deteriorated into powder, and inside the wool cloth, a considerable amount of this blaze-powder was gathered. A tiny bit had come out of the cloth, and it seemed that it stuck tightly to the glass ball, seeping into its surface and leaving a strange, mesmerizing tint to it.

Curious, I took the sachet of powder and opened it up, and placed one of the balls directly into the powder. It took a second for the powder to "realize" the ball was touching it, and all of a sudden, it moved of its own volition, rushing up and around the surface of the ball and covering it completely. The powder melted into the sphere, and when I could see the glassy surface again, it was vastly different.

The whole sphere seemed to weigh more, more than it by rights should for its size. Its surface seemed to slither just below the glass, giving the illusion that the ball was moving about when it was really still. It was a dark green color now, shimmering and shifting like milk in clear water. In the center, I could make out here and again the shape of an eye, seeming to dart about but not really focusing on anything. As I held it, my hands felt like they were buzzing, like an electric current ran through them.

I put the ball down, shook my hands a bit to get the feeling back in them. The ball rolled to one corner of the box, rested there as if it were actively trying to hide. I furrowed my brow at it, crossed my arms to consider it. My foot tapped the book I had left open on the floor, and, perhaps by chance but perhaps not, a tiny breeze that wafted through the room flipped the page.

There, on the paper, was a hand-drawn, detailed depiction of this very ball, surrounded in notes and diagrams. The page was titled, "The Key to the Plane of Darkness." My eyes widened, and I picked up the book, holding up the cipher key next to it and reading it on the fly.

"The Eye of the Ender seems to be the key to the gate which leads to the land of the Underworld, which we call the End. By itself, it is drawn to the portal, and will lead you toward the nearest temple of the End. Once you have found this portal, its twelve stone locks seem to fit the Eyes. I have, alas, only found three of these keys as of this writing. I know not what will happen if all twelve stone locks are filled, but it stands to reason that the gate should open, leading to this fell and terrible world."

Eyes of Ender . . . This man only found three, but I realized that I had possibly just discovered exactly how to make them myself! I held in my hand the very key to the End! I called the attention of Austin, Mary, and Anne, who were within earshot, and hastily explained my findings.

The news that there was believed to be a fourth place was overdone by the discovery that we now held what was very possibly a key to a hidden temple with a portal that led to the End. It was nearly noon, and we had no idea how far away the thing was or how long it would take to get there, but I proposed trying to let the Eye lead us to the temple right away. A resounding agreement was all I needed, and, with the thought of something so archaeologically significant as a "temple" within reach, the four of us scrambled down the elevator.

I held the ball up and waited. It happened so suddenly that I wasn't sure it happened at all, but I saw the eye inside suddenly lock in one direction, and the sphere's interior turned a deep, acid-like green. It leapt out of my hand and began speeding in mid-air to the east. We all took off after it. Katy and James would probably find the house empty and freak out, but at this moment in the venture, I don't think any of us had that thought register.

Through some trees, entering the jungle, Anne's voice sounded behind me. "This place . . . it looks similar to where I got lost a long time ago!" We kept running, vaulting over fallen logs and climbing up little ledges, deeper and deeper into the wood. I heard Anne swear. "There, that's the thing I saw!" she said.

Up ahead of us, I could see a dark shape rise up in the gloom. We were deep enough now in the jungle that the sun overhead was being blocked out by the thick canopy of leaves. The closer we got to this structure, the mossier and wetter the ground and surrounding stones and trees became. I could make out the outline of this place now—it was a sort of pyramidal, rounded building, almost like a mound of stone decorated into an important site.

A large opening, like a mouth in the face of a giant beast, loomed darkly in front of us. Inside, it was completely dark, and I could hear no sound.

The Eye stopped at the entrance of the temple and dropped to the soft ground, rolling benignly a bit before it came to rest, returned to its original, murky green and black state. I picked it up; it was cool to the touch.

Something strange about this place was apparent not only to me. Austin sucked a breath through his teeth. Meanwhile, Anne swore again to herself.

"I could have discovered this place ages ago, and I just missed it! Ugh, this is so frustrating!" She kicked the stone that formed the mouth of the cave. "You better believe we're coming back here tomorrow, we're bringing everyone with us, and we're going to tear your insides apart, you piece of junk!"

Austin started to clap slowly. Anne turned and smacked him.

We made our way back carefully, making sure to reverse-navigate for easy rediscovery of the structure. The tree house was lit up, and I could see people moving inside, so I assumed the other two got home.

When we rode the elevator up, James was making a frame with his hands, looking through them to where Katy was arranging something on a stand. "What's up, you guys—" I began, before I realized what Katy was doing.

Katy had sculpted a sort of stand, a T-shape on the wooden floor, out of the sticky black sand we'd gathered from the Nether. She had the book we'd left here in one hand and was placing one of the terrible black skulls in the center of the other two skulls.

It was already too late. Katy turned and saw us.

"Welcome back! Do you like the new art piece? I copied it from the book because it looked cool."

I took a deep breath. "We need to get out of this house, now. Grab anything valuable you can hold, and move. NOW!"

That page of the book was not yet transliterated, but I'd read over it. Katie had just summoned the Wither.

# Of Dragons and Demons

It was already too late. I shut my eyes hard, took a deep breath. No stopping it now.

"Listen, everyone. Grab anything of value, anything you can jam in a bag in the next thirty seconds, and get out of the house."

Katy looked at me funny. "What? What did I do?"

"Just GO!" I said and darted to a chest, lifting the entire box off the ground and slamming it onto the elevator platform. Austin seemed to understand the gravitas of the situation and scrambled to get another box. James dumped several things off of shelves into a bag, and we all gathered as much as we could onto the elevator. Austin pulled the switch, and we began to rapidly descend just as the rumbling, buzzing sound began.

It was a sort of sound that you *felt* before you heard it, like it resonated in your lungs and flowed outward. It started low, like a bass note that you could only barely perceive, but then as it grew in intensity, it became almost ear-shattering in its whining pitch. I winced.

"Grab weapons. Leave this stuff here, we need to—"

The house above us exploded into thousands of splinters and shards of wood. As the debris rained down on top of us, I covered my head with my arms and ran out, away from the jungle. "FOLLOW ME!" I shouted, and, with that seeming like the best course of action, the others followed me. I indexed the weapons I had in my head.

The book talked about what this thing was, where it was from, and how to bring it to this plane. It did not talk about how to kill it. I swore loudly and repeatedly as we darted toward the plains, the most open piece of landscape nearby.

A hissing, echoing voice sounded from behind us, the sort of sound that chilled you to your bones.

"*Wheeere isss the draaaagooooon?*" it said. "*Wheeere isss iiit?*"

From the trees where our house once hung arose a huge, nightmarish creature. The pictures in the book did not do it justice. It seemed to hover in the air, its body a black that absorbed all the light around it. Black smoke spun around it in a tornado shape, seeming to ignite in little patches here and there inside. Its body was long and snake-like, skeletal, with no visible flesh on it anywhere and only jagged ribs protruding from an elongated spinal column that swayed and slithered in the air. It seemed to drip a thick tar-like substance from its bones.

On the top of this body was a three-pronged neck, terminating in three terrible black skulls, mouths gaping open and shining with a sinister grey light from the mouths and eyes. Clouds around the Wither began to swirl and get pulled into the tornado like smoke spinning around it. Up above, the sky, which was already darkened with clouds, seemed to groan under the strain of keeping up appearances, and a thunderclap resounded.

"First the house gets blown up, then the Wither appears, and now it's going to rain," I said under my breath and kept running. The plains had a few hills on them, so we might be able to take better cover behind the mounds of earth than the flimsy leafy canopy cover that the jungle would provide.

As the first drops of rain began falling, the Wither turned its attention toward us.

"*Whattt isss thisss? Whooo hasss sssummoned meee?*" it hissed, and with a speed I did not expect, it flew through the air directly toward us. The center mouth opened wider, and a sort of coughing sound emitted from it, followed by the expulsion of a black projectile.

It had spit a skull at us. As if a skeleton-snake-nightmare wasn't bad enough! It had to make things worse! It had to spit MORE SKULLS at us. The skull flew in a straight line, its mouth opening and closing as it flew, its black eye sockets empty and hollow with a flack flame trailing behind it.

"James! Watch out!" cried Katy and reached out to try to grab him and pull him out of the way. She was just a second too late, though, and the skull crashed into James' back, exploding into a black smoke that swirled around him and seemed to absorb into his skin. His eyes bugged out, and he coughed suddenly and intensely, spitting up some black, sludge-like fluid.

No time, no time! Get to cover, *then* deal with the injured James! We dragged him around one of the small hills and laid him back. "You deal with James!" I said to Katy, drew out my bow, and popped up over the top of the mound, aiming only briefly before firing. The arrow sped toward the Wither and disappeared into the black smoke. Instantly, the thing recoiled and then hissed loudly again, launching another of its terrible, black skulls at me. I managed to duck under the mound before it hit me.

"Arrows work! Use arrows!" I said hoarsely. Everyone who had a bow fitted an arrow. The Wither flew over and stopped directly above us and opened all three of its mouths. As if we'd had it planned, four arrows rocketed upward, all four striking the nightmare at once before it could spit more skulls at us, and it shuddered, retreating a few meters.

"*Fooolsss!*" it hissed and spat more skulls at our earthen barrier. James had become pale and weak, and his face had lost all color. His breathing was erratic. Katie frantically tried to help him, tried to figure out what to do. He pointed weakly to his throat and made a dry, rasping sound, and so she rather hysterically grabbed up her milk skin and pulled the cap off, putting it to his lips and letting the liquid drain into his lips. He sputtered a bit, but the milk trickled down his throat and into his stomach.

Meanwhile, Austin took charge of the fight. "Vincent, you and I go left. Mary, Anne, you go right. Barrage it from both sides. Go, now!" I ran with my head down to the left, following Austin, and launched arrows as best I could while moving. Mary's arrows were faster and plunged into the Wither with more power and accuracy. It forced the Wither back toward Austin and me, and Anne continued firing on with her flaming arrows as well. The closer it got to the two of us, the more arrows we put into it. It did not seem to have expected to meet such resistance as the likes of us, as it seemed to be simultaneously trying to blindly attack us with the skulls and trying to figure out what would be a better way of attacking us.

"It said 'dragon.' What dragon? The dragon in the End?" shouted Austin over the crashing and exploding of the Wither's projectiles.

James blinked hard, coughed up another gobbet of the black sooty gunk. The color returned to his cheeks, and he shook his head. "The hell was—"

"No time, start shooting," said Katy, pulling out her bow. We had the Wither pinned down from three sides, arrows coming in a nonstop stream. Or, at least, we did. I ran out of arrows, and only a few seconds later, so did Austin. To make it worse, the sun just dipped below the horizon. Here we were out in the open, fighting a hugely destructive monster that was tearing holes in the countryside with its deadly and explosive skulls, and now it was night. That meant the *other* monsters would come out.

"I'm out of arrows!" I heard someone yell. This was not the way to die, summoning an eldritch horror of the sky on *accident* and then dying because we ran out of arrows. I racked my brain for a plan.

Just then, I heard the low, ghoulish moan of the first zombie coming into the plain. A skeleton appeared over the crest of the taller hill in the plain. Its bow was old and worn, but it was still deadly. I saw it fit an arrow to its string.

That! That was it! That skeleton had a full quiver of arrows there. I steeled myself and dashed for the hill. My movement caught the attention of the Wither, and it turned toward me, opening one of its mouths.

"*Unnnwissse, mortalll . . .*" it said in its snake-like voice and inhaled deeply. I barreled headlong into the skeleton, dodging its first arrow and not giving it a chance to nock another. Axe out, head severed from neck bones, quiver of arrows in hand. Good.

As if to mock me, I heard a soft footfall behind me and turned, face-to-face with a green mottled creature with an angry-looking countenance seemingly painted onto its bulbous head. The thunder crackled overhead.

Think, Vincent. *Think*. The Wither gasped and spat the skull it had prepared—but not at me. No, the skull was aimed . . .

At the Creeper? It turned its sickening green-scaled head and stepped back just in time to avoid the projectile just as I smelled the gathering ozone. The Wither's eyes locked onto the Creeper, and it seemed to phase forward in the air toward the green beast. The Creeper glowed momentarily and began emitting a sort of hissing noise, indicative of its decision. I lifted my axe, slammed it down on top of the Creeper's head, and dove backward down the side of the hill.

CRASH! A stroke of lightning came down on the metal axe, which was still buried in the Creeper's head. The electricity shot through its body, and it suddenly shone with a bright blue light. The Wither collided with it full-force and lifted it off the ground just as the creeper, charged with the energy from the lightning, exploded in a full-force display of just how terrible fire can be. The two creatures disappeared in the blast, and I, who had rolled down the hill some, covered my head with my arms as the flash's wave of heat rolled over me. The entire hill shifted, and I felt myself hurtling backwards as the shock wave finally came. When the smoke cleared, all that was left of the two creatures was a huge white crystalline star, the size of my entire torso, that held in the air for a moment before drifting down to the ground.

Anne called over the noise. "Vincent! Are you okay?"

I struggled to my feet and staggered, running as best I could back toward the old shelter. "Ask me when we are safe!" I called back, and, mowing down a zombie or two on the way, we all arrived back at Anne's laboratory. She shut the door behind us, and pushed a worktable up against it to keep it closed.

"What was that?" gasped Katy. "I am so sorry, I had no idea—"

"Not now," said Anne. She pushed a button on the wall, and a panel in the floor opened up, the inside rising out of the opening to be a table of medical supplies. "Medical first. Injuries?" Anne spent a few minutes fixing up James and me, miraculously the only two of us that were injured. James still looked a little sick, but he said he wasn't dying like when the skull hit him.

"It was like all my insides had suddenly shriveled up," he described it. "Like the skull had drawn all the water out of me and was trying to turn me into dust. I could feel it creeping further into my veins the whole time. It was oppressive. I can't explain it better than with that word. Katy here gave me something to drink, though. I think I might have died without that."

I thought about the star-looking item that fell from the Wither. "Should we pick that thing up?" I posited. "I mean, it came from the Wither, and we've had good luck picking up items that monsters have left when we killed them. We found the temple with the combination of the rod from that blaze monster and the pearl from the black thing. What is to say that thing will not have some use?"

Katy looked somber for a long while. Her face was downcast, and she didn't talk. She said later she was afraid that we would be angry at her for summoning what amounted to be a demon that destroyed our house and everything left in it, which I supposed was a fair assumption. I mean, after all, that was literally what she did.

All things considered, though, none of *us* were really injured, and we had managed to save a great deal of our stuff. I do not think any of us were terribly upset, at least at the moment. We were too busy being alive to be angry. The tension in the little laboratory was high enough, however, that we stationed a watch that night. Katy volunteered to go first, and then it was me.

When it was my turn, I sat and stared out the window in the dark.

The usual fare crossed my field of vision here and again—great big spiders, skeletons holding their ancient bows, green-skinned walking dead that groaned as they shuffled along the dirt. Now and again I would see a wildcat scurry across the beach back toward the forest. I wondered just what else was there out there that we didn't know. What would we see in the temple when we went to explore it? Would they be allies? Enemies? I simply didn't know.

We waited until the sun was high in the sky the next day before we went outside. The remains of the skeletons and zombies that were caught in the sunlight dotted the landscape as the six of us trekked toward the site of the destruction to inspect that star. In the light, the destruction that the Wither had caused was all too apparent. Giant holes in the ground, the loose dirt scattered around them, the hill on which the Creeper and the Wither met their end, little fragments of bone and soot from where our arrows pierced the monster. Mary scrounged in the dirt of the hill for a second and stood back up lugging the star.

We carried it to the laboratory and set it on a worktable. Anne put a glass case over it, and we left it there for the time being. What we needed to do was get our house back up, better and safer than before. Mary and I went to inspect the damage done to the house.

True to the sound we heard and the explosion we saw, there was barely a shred left of the house. The elevator and the things we'd left on it were all safe and undamaged, but the tree itself was completely wrecked. The entire top portion of the once-mighty trunk had been blasted into oblivion and with it several of the branches of neighboring trees. If we were to look for a place to rebuild the house, it most certainly would not be here. Mary kicked at a piece of the splintered wood and chuckled ironically.

"We put it up there so it would be safer, so Creepers would not be able to blow it up. Instead, it gets blown up from the inside. We're good at this," she said, tapping on her head. I grinned.

"So we make a better house somewhere else. What about out in the water? Make a floating structure. It would take some time to build, certainly, but as long as we have a safe place to return to at night, we can make it work fine." I picked up a metal boot from the stack of items on the elevator and overturned it, dumping out the rainwater that had collected the night before.

We spent the next few days discussing where to build the new safe house. It was decided that we would use hard stone blocks rather than cobblestone, because they seemed stronger. It was also decided, perhaps foolhardily, that we would build the new house underwater. If the ground was not safe and the air was not safe, then there left only the water, and as far as we knew it, only squids and fish lived in the water. On occasion, one might see a zombie trying to swim in it, but they only lasted until the holes in their bodies filled up with water and they sank to the bottom.

We built a large bank of smelting furnaces to create the large amounts of glass we would need to make the walls of our underwater miniature city. The plans we drew up were huge. An entire wing of the compound would be Austin's farm, which he would transplant there. Another would be a sort of museum-gallery where the art pieces that we made would be displayed (within reason, of course, specified Katy, still embarrassed by the entire ordeal). A third wing would house us with food facilities and sleeping quarters. The fourth wing would be our armory; this is where we would store and organize weaponry and magical items for use in defeating whatever came our way.

We were highly aware of the fact that we did not belong underwater and could only hold breath for a short time, so we first built a floating platform above where we intended to have the central hub. From there we would take turns diving into the water, clearing away the unnecessary earth and stone, and then coming back up for breath. It was slow work, but it was actually quite entertaining. The fish that swam around in the water seemed curious at what we were doing, and the black squids came closer to inspect our work after we came up for air. James, who did not feel confident in his ability to swim, stayed on the shoreline and tended the furnace bank, making sheet after sheet of heavy, thick glass out of the fine, clean sand that washed up on the beach. Now and again he'd find some little trinket in the sand, a shell of some tiny creature or the like.

It was only when his shovel hit something hard and stony that he paused in his work. He dusted off the stone his shovel had clanged against. It was a sort of cobblestone itself, but it was laced with a kind of green moss. He cleared away more of the sand around it to find that there was a large square of the mossy cobblestone, almost like the roof of a small room. Intrigued, he fetched a pickaxe and broke open a small hole in the top.

Inside the small room, which seemed to have no entrances or exits, there was just a single stone pedestal, into which was jammed a glittering diamond sword. James dropped inside the room, alighting on the floor that was oddly clean for having not been opened for quite a long time, and approached this sword. There was a plaque on the stone pedestal. It read:

"Here lieth the sword of the Great Hero, who slew the Fell Beast Wither, who rid the land of the Plague-Stricken Citizens. Though he now lieth in the womb of the earth, this sword beareth his legacy and his name."

Hesitantly, James wrapped his fingers around the hilt of the blade. He pulled it upward, and it slid free of the stone pillar. It was light in his hand, and its edge glinted in the low light. He scrutinized the blade for a second before sliding it into his belt and climbing back out of the hole.

Back up on the surface, he shook his head. As if they hadn't had enough proof that there was a culture here long ago, more and more archaeological artifacts keep showing up. He'd have to make sure to tell the others when they got back from their offshore work.

Meanwhile, the rest of us were taking turns diving down into the water, holding our breath as long as we could, and flattening the ground under us. When it came time for the walls to begin being built, we started paddling the great platform back toward land. James met us at the shoreline, caught the rope we threw to him, and anchored it around a stone.

"You'll never guess what I have found," he said and pointed to the sword, which was sticking into a pile of sand and glittering in the sun.

For the next two weeks, our schedule was wake up in the morning, work on the new compound, hang out at night, go to bed. We made quite a lot of progress, even transplanting Austin's entire greenhouse farm to the underwater wing. When we were finished with this compound, it had a similar elevator to the one that had led us to the tree, but this one took a platform from the shore out several meters into the water horizontally before descending into a glass tunnel that deposited you in the central hub, where just for fun Anne and Mary built a fountain out of glass and gold.

Following the instructions in the book left by the explorer, we built an obsidian table with a red cloth over it, on top of which we placed a blank book. The instructions said that this was a place where one could use one's own energy, one's own power to infuse objects with magic much in the same way that the magic books we had could be used with an anvil. The notes mentioned that the more books were placed around it, the stronger the magic could be, but we only had so few books.

Next up was the armory. From our mining efforts from before, we had gathered quite a lot of iron ore, from which we let James operate the furnaces to smelt the usable iron. From that point, it was a simple matter to hammer the metal into the shapes we needed—helmets, swords, boots, breastplates, tools of all kinds. Katy, who was particularly handy with a hammer, banged away at the worktables and anvils until each of us had a full set of iron armor, a full set of tools, a sword and a bow to complete the set.

Finally, we moved Katy's laboratory into the space not taken up by Austin's farm. In a bigger space, now, she expanded her work to have multiple project tables at one time. All in all, this new house was quite an improvement. It was safer, as it was deep underwater, and it was bigger and roomier, and better-designed architecturally. It offered a good defense against the outside world.

We sat in the lounge, discussing over cups of milk and slices of pumpkin pie the next steps. We could try to find a use for the huge star gem, or we could go to explore that temple in the jungle. We could try to storm the stronghold in the Nether and get more of those rods from the blazes to combine with the pearls we already had to make more of the keys to the End. We had quite a bit to do.

Fortunately, because Mary and I had been through the stronghold before, we could guide the others there far more easily than when we had done it. Added to our fortune was that there was a distinct lack of ghast in the air to ruin our day, and we arrived in the stronghold with no problems. We were prepared not only for the normal skeletons and the blazes but also for the taller, bigger, black skeletons that Mary and I now could place as being related to the Wither. The whole aura about them was similar, if perhaps less in intensity, to the Wither, and it only made sense now, seeing as it was indeed the skulls of these monsters that were required for the summoning of the Wither in the first place.

The only real advantage that the blazes had now was their range, but we matched that with bows. Their surprise factor was broken after you'd seen it once. And when the footsteps began coming through the halls, this time, *we* waited in ambush for it. Even with its great stone sword, it did not have the time to strike one blow before it was reduced to rubble. As a point of spite, we took its skull and jammed it into our bag. We spent several hours in the Nether, having built a tiny room to retreat to and rest in whenever we were tired or injured. By the end of the day, we'd acquired ten or eleven Blaze's rods, three black Wither skulls, and several bloated, grey-red mushrooms that we'd never seen before. With the dust that these rods would produce, we'd have more than enough to make the rest of the pearls into Eyes of Ender.

Back at the underwater compound, which we'd started to refer to as "the Tetrapus," we planned out our next expedition: into the jungle temple.

I mused. "It's amazing how terrifying something is the first time, but then the second time you see it," I started.

"It's like you've already seen it once, so it's not even remotely scary, right?" Mary finished. "And when you bring along reinforcements, it makes the whole ordeal seem like a cakewalk." She balanced her piece of cake on her head and took a few steps for fun, and we all laughed.

The venture into the temple was to be a two-day venture, first day mapping and second day looting. If we found this portal to the End, like the book said we would, then all the better! We would know where to go when we were prepared to go to this dark plane.

Anne was fired up more than anyone else for it. She and this thing had a history, for sure. It was decided that she would take the initiative and lead point. This being the third new place we would have gone to explore, we took the correct hints and packed appropriately: customized suits of armor, proper tools, weapons that glowed with magic. We would not be surprised again by anything like we were before.

That day, as we stood at the entrance to the temple in the jungle, the sky was clear, and the jungle's ambient sounds were unmarred by monsters or beasts. The mouth of the temple gaped at us, empty and dark, vines and vegetation growing into the cracks in the stone bricks. We would take this like we had taken the mines, same procedure with a different place.

The halls of this temple were made of a sort of moss-covered, wet stone brick, held together fast by mortar. As we ventured in further, we found old torches still burning in the damp air that illuminated the pathways, and, more disconcertingly, shuffling footprints that crossed over each other, relatively fresh-looking. Zombies, I thought, and possibly skeletons as well, but then, they hadn't really been a problem since the beginning, when they had first showed up.

Anne turned a corner and stopped short.

"Guys, take a look at this," she said, motioning us inside.

The walls of this room were cracked brick, crumbling and mossy, and had thick metal bars set into the ground, a metal door locked tightly against them. This room contained *prison cells*. Two of them, facing each other, with the previous inhabitants of the cells evidently still in them. Bones lie scattered on the stone floor, surrounded by mysterious scratches and stains. The very metal bars seemed to have been chewed upon near the floor, as gnaw marks were evident on the surface of the iron a few inches off the ground, obviously not done by any human teeth.

I shuddered. On the walls, there were huge metal buttons. Hesitantly, Anne pushed one of them, and as we all expected, the door to its side swung open. A minute or two later, it slammed shut.

"This is a temple?" murmured Austin. "No temple I have ever heard of would have prison cells in it . . ."

James nodded in agreement. "What if this religion used human sacrifice?"

It dawned on me at that point, though I did not know it had. The thought-seed was planted and began to grow, to worm its roots into my brain. What if . . . the monsters—

Mary alerted us to something in the hallway. "Incoming, you guys! And a *lot* of them!" She drew out her bow and backed up a few steps, letting arrows fly. "A *LOT* of them!"

She was right. As though we had tripped some sort of alarm system, around the corner came a veritable horde of the undead. Far too many for my taste. What's worse, some of them were carrying weaponry, old, broken-looking swords and axes, or wearing tattered and damaged armor. Moaning through the openings of the helmets, they shuffled in a huge clump down the hallway.

Think fast. Could we take them? No, we could not take this many of them, all at once. One at a time, certainly, that would be simple, but getting surrounded would be tantamount to suicide. Okay, so we thin the herd a bit, I thought. Can we bottleneck them? No, the rooms did not have doorways, just turns in the hallway. Could we use a corner to our advantage? If we could somehow trick them into thinking we were somewhere else . . .

That was it! I unslung my pickaxe. "Keep them busy for a minute!" I cried, pushing open one of the prison cell doors and ducking inside. I began my attack on the wall, the pickaxe cleanly pulling apart the bricks in the walls until I had a considerably sized narrow passage, In the hallway, I heard the thuds of arrows and the cutting of swords mingle with the moaning and gasping of the zombies. Just a few more seconds! I kept picking at the wall as fast as I could and finally broke out into another hallway, one we'd already passed through as evidenced by the marks we left on the walls. Perfect!

I spun around and pulled out some wooden planks. "Everyone! Run into the prison cell!"

"*What?*" Mary cried back.

"Just trust me! Open the cell and run inside!" I prepared to jam the wooden planks into the narrow walkway as soon as they came past. One, two, three, four, all five past me, and not a second to spare! The horde began shuffling into the cell, trying to press into the hole in the wall, but I smashed the planks down hard and kicked them into position, jamming them across the walkway. I pushed the pile of broken stone up against the back of the boards as the zombies suddenly found themselves unable to move forward. They crowded into the cell, trying to reach us as we stood securely in the open hallway. More and more of them forced themselves into the cell, until there was absolutely no more possible space for them to move, and then . . .

*Clang!* The heavy metal door behind them swung shut loudly. We barred the tiny walkway up as best we could with the broken stones and wooden planks and then circled around back to the entrances of the cells. The bars held fast. We were at least safe from this mob.

The green-skinned once-humans pushed and groaned against the metal bars, arms extending between them as if to cry out for help, for freedom. We knew better.

We continued on the same path, heading up the hall down which the horde had come. It turned and hit a 4-way intersection of halls. To one direction, there seemed to be a balcony. To another, there was a staircase going downward, and to still another, there was only another turn in the hallway. Anne motioned toward the balcony, and we hurried that direction.

The balcony was actually a mezzanine overhanging the first floor of a huge library. This second floor's walls were also packed to the brim with books, their spines faded and covered with cobwebs. Austin hazarded to pick up one of the books of the shelf. As he pulled it out, we all tensed up, waiting for the telltale click of a trap being set off.

None came. There was a unanimous sigh of relief as he dusted off the blank cover and then opened up the pages. The whole book was written in that cipher script, like Pollus' book, and there were no illustrations. So was the next one, and so was the next. These books must have been old, older than even when Pollus came.

The center of the floor below us was cleared, surrounded by bookshelves. The floor was an almost-polished, shiny marble covered in a layer of ancient dust, unmarred by footprints like the ones we encountered in the hallway. Smack dab in the middle was another obsidian table much like the one we had built but far older and far more used, it seemed. The corners of the black stone were worn down smooth over years and years of use, and the book that floated above the table, slowly rotating in the dim light from the torches in the walls, was fat and thick, as though it had eaten many of the other books.

And so it had; looking closely, I noticed that the books on the shelves around it seemed to be loose in their spines, as though pages had been torn out of the hard covers and thrown away. Even more thrilling, though, was what was happening in the air around this book.

From books all around the center table, little droplets of ink dripped out of the pages. I thought of the term, 'dripped,' because there was no better word to describe it, though even that fell short, but they did not drip toward the floor like they should have. No, they dripped toward the center book. Droplets of the black ink slipped out and flew toward the great tome, slowly enough to notice that they formed the shape of the glyphs from that writing system in the air before splashing into the book's own pages, being absorbed in less than a second into its white pages. How long had this book been devouring the very words from these other books?

I swung myself over the railing of the balcony and dropped down onto the lower floor. The air became heavy, almost electric the closer I got to the enchanting tome. I heard someone utter a warning behind me, but I wasn't paying attention. No, my eyes were set on this book. I took another step toward it, and the book suddenly turned to face its pages toward me, as if waiting for me to take another step.

The cover of the book burst open, and the pages fluttered before my eyes. They came to rest on a page with only one line of text in the center. The cipher trickled through my brain again as I deciphered the line on sight:

"Welcome, explorer."

I shook my head. "You guys, this book knows we are here," I called back.

"What?" I heard James say. "Is the book alive or something?"

The page turned, and I read it aloud. "I neither live nor go without life."

One by one, James, Katy, Anne, Austin, and Mary dropped down to this floor. When Katy came close, however, the book violently fluttered its pages and spun around. Alarmed, she jumped back, and the book calmed down.

On the page were the words, "You and only you shall be permitted." I relayed this to the others. Austin half-smirked.

"What are you, the chosen one?" he said with a laugh.

The book responded, "Yes."

I stared at the pages as they turned themselves.

"Listen closely, explorer, and I will tell you all you wish to know." I read the pages out loud. "This place is, as you thought, a temple. Long, long ago, there lived a people who extolled the sovereignty of the great Ender Dragon, who once terrorized the skies of this world. The Dragon required tribute in the form of blood, the blood of heroes. Thusly, you will find further inside this temple the remains of an arena where they would bring their warriors to fight in gladiatorial matches to test their hearts and find the heroes to sacrifice.

"This violent and bloody civilization flourished in this land, and its workers pressed far underground to find the resources that they needed to keep the gladiators fighting. Those that would not fight were forced to work, and those that would not or could not work were used in the bloody rituals for the Dragon.

"Then one day, a man in a black helmet with a shining sword appeared, and with no effort, he defeated all the greatest gladiators. When the Dragon came to claim its tribute of this great fighter, the man summoned a great beast from the fiery realm of the Nether, and the two beasts fought. They fought for days on end, a great, glistening, three-headed snake whose body was as fast as the river is wide, and a gargantuan, lizard-like creature with great, leathery wings. The black-helmed man rode on the back of his beast and ruthlessly attacked the Dragon with his shining sword.

"But the Dragon would not be fetched a turn by this black and red hell-serpent, and with a great breath, he covered the Serpent of the Nether in black fire and burned away its flesh, leaving nothing but bone. In this moment, when the fight seemed to be over, the black-helmed man held his sword up high and cut a hole in the very air into a world that was only black. The hole drew the dragon and the hero inside, leaving his sword behind in the wake.

"But the bones of the Serpent of the Nether would not lie still. Though the people buried them out of fear, they rose out of their grave on the next full moon. This skeletal serpent became violent and uncontrollable and began to destroy the city and devour whole the people who confronted it. It seemed to siphon the very life from its victims, and those who fought it were left dry, brittle corpses. None could stand against it.

"Until, in a stroke of emergent necessity, a young boy seized the gleaming sword that once belonged to the hero and turned, severing the Wither's three heads all in one fell sweep. The bones turned to dust immediately, and all that was left was a jewel in the shape of a star. The legends say that whoever uses the Nether Star with the correct offering can gain the power needed to slay the Ender Dragon once and for all.

"The boy became the city's new hero and continued the legacy of the one who disappeared into the dark rift with the Dragon. Where the rift had been cut, all that was left was a hole in the ground that burned with molten stone that would never cool. The priests of the city built a shrine around it and theorized for years about how to open the hole again and return the hero to this world.

"Thus, you found Pollus' tome detailing the Eyes of Ender and the keys to the Gate of the End. Do you understand?"

We had blocked up all the entryways into the room with the heavy shelves of books and made camp there for the night. A cooking fire burned on the stone floor, and we all sat around it, out of the reach of the book's mind-reading.

Quite a lot of information was revealed to us. The monsters we fought so routinely were indeed the previous inhabitants of the civilization that lived here, but they were only the ones which were killed for the sake of or directly by the Ender Dragon and tainted by its evil. The Ender-Men, as the black abominations were called, were the souls of the ones killed that the dragon had eaten, escaping from the End and taking form in the world they once knew. All that we did not now know was anything about this fourth realm, the Sky World.

The Book claimed to know nothing about it, aside from the fact that it existed, or perhaps had existed at one point. Why the book would only allow me anywhere near it was beyond me, but at the least, it did not seem malevolent.

Katy poked at the fire with a stick then turned over the beef which was roasting above it. "So, the Wither wants to destroy the Ender Dragon. The Ender Dragon is what is causing the remains of the people to continue to rise up and roam the earth. Do you think we're meant to kill the Dragon?"

Anne shook her head. "I don't believe in destiny. What I do think is that even with this magic sword, we are not heroes. I don't think we can kill a god."

"We killed the Wither," James piped up.

"No, a Creeper and a lucky strike of lightning killed the Wither. We barely even scratched it. We haven't got a single chance," she replied. "I think we're better off dealing with the monsters as they appear than trying to enter a portal to a world where, as far as we know, only Ender-Men and the Dragon live. I wouldn't set a single foot in that place if I could avoid it."

We were silent again for a short while, the consideration weighing in on us. What if we did go to fight the dragon? Would we be killed? How would we fight it? The book said that the Nether Star would grant us the power to defeat the Dragon if we could figure out how and where to use it, but how long would it take us to figure that out?

We had a theoretically infinite amount of time, but then, the last thing that the book said before I retreated from it still stuck in my mind. I hadn't told the others when I read it..

"The Wither seeks your head now, as well, but it seeks the head of the Ender Dragon more. Unless you put an end to the Dragon and soon, the Wither will regenerate and force its way back into this world, and it will find you.

"And it will kill all of you, one by one, starting with you, if you do not slay the Dragon yourself."

Had I told them, surely Katy would take the blame on herself now that there was a terrible god from the realm of the dead that sought to bring us home with it, and I did not want her to bear that burden. But then, what must I do to bring the matter of the killing of the dragon to bear on my comrades?

"I think we need some time to prepare, if anything. Get as much magic as we can muster, and make sure that we understand all of it. See if we cannot gain an edge against the Dragon. See if we cannot figure out the Wither Star." I pulled a chunk of the roasted meat from the spit and chewed on it. "It seems like putting an end to the Dragon would be in the best interests of this whole world. If we can stop it, then I say we should try."

Anne just shook her head again. "We are dealing with gods here, Vincent. We cannot even think to stand against a god."

The book had told us who Pollus was, as well. It said Pollus was a traveler from far across the sea, much like us, who had been exiled from his own civilization. They were pacifists, the whole of them, and Pollus was one of the very few who advocated the active defense of their colony from the monsters that plagued it. Their monsters were giant creatures, wolf-like behemoths and spiders that stood as tall as horses, but because his people were peace-loving and revered all life, they would constantly come under attack from these huge beasts and many would lose their lives. He was exiled because his thoughts were too war-like, and so he took it upon himself to become an explorer. He got in a boat and simply sailed until he came to new land.

Pollus was an accomplished magician in his own right, so when he discovered the magic of this civilization, he mixed it with his own knowledge. That was where the separation came from in the writing: the script he used, which is the script we all knew, came from far beyond the sea, and the script they used here was completely different, but he managed to be able to translate it and use it in his own magic.

The book refused to speak, however, about itself. It was clear to me, at least, that this book was once a human and that somehow that person's thoughts and mind were bound to this book. The book, however, insisted that it was never human and was simply a book of great magical power. It said something peculiar, there:

"I am not like those failed marriages of science and magic that now seed the dark places of the earth." It would not elaborate on that point, almost as if it had not intended to say it. I believed further with every sentence the book spit out that it was once a human being.

Everyone had eaten their fill, and a guard rotation had been established. Even with the heavy shelves blocking all the ways in, there was still no assurance that we would not be sneak-attacked by something from a secret panel. When it was my watch, I took it with the book again.

"Tell me everything you can tell me about the Ender Dragon. If I am to try to fight it, I must know how to do so," I whispered into the pages.

The text on the page said, "I cannot see into the Dark Realm, but during the moment when the rift was open, I could see the inside. There were towers of black stone, on top of which were great burning crystals. They seemed to reach out to the Dragon and welcome it back. I also saw that there was an infinity below the island on which the Dragon resides, and an infinity above it. Thousands of Ender-Men's eyes blinked from the vast expanse of floating islands inside.

"It is my best assumption that the dark world there is where the Dragon was born and that somehow it came to this world long ago. That it has not come back again is a statement of its inability to control its imprisonment, and for that the people of this land were grateful. Even after it was gone, though, they still continued the gladiatorial games, and that produced more of the living dead.

"This is all I know."

"Teach me more magic," I whispered.

"That, my dear explorer, I can do!"

By the end of my watch period, my eyes stung and burned, and my body begged for rest, but my mind was heavy with the knowledge that the book imparted onto me. It was as if the text has opened the door to my mind and poured in such arcane and eldritch knowledge as I had never even dreamed and then closed the door and shook it all up. I was aware of James saying something to me in passing to take his place as the watch, but I was unconscious before I even hit the floor.

My dreams were filled with incantations and strange glyphs.

The next morning, I awoke to find the other five sleeping fitfully, the remains of the fire died out. Anne, whose turn it had been to watch, had fallen asleep on a pile of books, which she had built up to sit upon. I shook my head and rubbed my eyes; I needed to be awake.

I went to the book. "Magic. Now. I need protection from fire. I need protection from falling. I need lots and lots of protection. Let's make this armor as magic as it can get."

The book's page turned. "At your service."

I had dreamed it. I had dreamed that everyone else had been killed. I had dreamed that if I did not go and slay the Dragon myself, the Wither would appear when we least expected it, and it would drain everyone to death. There wasn't time to even debate about it. I dreamed that everyone was dead, that I was the first to die and that the Dragon had killed us. I dreamed that when the six of us gathered together and raised arms against the Dragon, it had immediately killed all of us. I dreamed that the Wither and the Dragon both laughed as we fell into hell.

That was not going to happen on my watch. If the destiny described insisted that I had to do it alone, as the "chosen one," like the book said, then by the stars, I would end that Dragon faster than a lit match could burn out in a rainstorm. I had to go alone, so I had to be stealthy.

I set all the Eyes into the frame of the portal, the location of which was easy to discern from the art on the walls, paintings of the very scene of the Hero and the Dragon being sucked into the void. As the last eye set inside, all of them at once shifted to look toward the inside of the portal, a stone circle hovering over a pit of lava.

If I did not go now, the others would wake, would find me missing, and would follow me. I had to go now. I had taken James's sword and Mary's bow, and with my armor positively radiating magic, I felt like I had a chance. I took a deep breath and jumped.

The sensation wasn't unlike that of passing through the portal into the Nether, but this one seemed to take longer and twist my insides even more. It spit me out violently onto a hard, black and gray stone surface, and I tumbled a few feet when I hit the ground. I sprang back to my feet, though, and my hand was immediately on my sword. If I was going to do this alone, then I was going to do it with everything I had.

The muted black and grey landscape around me assaulted my senses, almost as if my entire vision had been greyscaled. The only color I could see was on myself and from the shining stones atop the tall black towers that jutted up from the ground like spears. They pulsed with a sort of purplish energy, an energy that reminded me of the open mouths of the Ender-men when we fought them in waves at our home.

It wasn't coincidental. Dozens of floating islands hung stationary in the air, and on those islands, at least a hundred Ender-men stood or shuffled about lazily, carrying thick blocks of the black stone or just sauntering and staring. I searched the terrain for the Dragon, the great, fell lizard I knew was here somewhere. Up ahead, there seemed to be a raised plateau. I made my way that direction.

The silence in this place was broken only by the throaty, grunting noises of the Ender-men, but as I came closer to the plateau, I heard a sort of rhythmic, rasping sound, slow and hissy.

Breathing.

The ground around the plateau sloped upward to meet the top of its flat surface, and I found as I climbed that my heart raced faster and faster. The breathing was almost thunderous now, and as I reached the top of the slope, I saw the terrifying shape of the Ender Dragon, coiled up on its haunches.

I stood resolutely, my sword in my hand. The Dragon turned its head and regarded me.

*"Too long has it been since last I saw your kind. Have you come to try to slay me, little hero?"* it said, in a voice that boomed through the silence.

I pointed my sword at it. "You remember this blade, don't you?" I said, and the blade gleamed in the low light. "It did you in once, and it is here to finish the job."

*"Let us not make talk, then, little hero. Come, and face your permanent destiny."* The dragon's sinister smile belied its calm demeanor, and it lifted its huge form off the ground, standing at its full height. *"I will show you the true meaning of fear."* With a flap of its great wings, it shot up into the air, and circled around the plateau.

As it approached the gems, the pulses of energy seemed to leap from the stones and into the body of the dragon. I watched it seem to devour this energy, and its body looked as though it were growing stronger. I had no time to lose.

The dragon swooped down dramatically, its wings spread wide, and opened its jaws, as if to catch me up and bite me in half. I leapt to the side, bringing the shimmering blade up as hard as I could into the leathery skin covering the dragon's wings. It tore easily through the webbing, and the dragon wailed loudly, landing on the ground and skidding in the stone.

Then it began to laugh, a terrible, crazy laugh. I watched it hold its injured wing up, and the closest crystal shot a beam of the purple energy down onto it. Before my very eyes, the wound I had struck began to knit itself back together, leathery skin reforming into an unblemished surface.

*"Now you see? You have no power! You have no chance! You are DUST to me!"* it shouted deafeningly. Its calm demeanor from before was suddenly replaced with a lower, more ragged voice, a voice of someone who had taken off their gloves and begun to play the game for keeps. I swore to myself and kept my eyes resolute. It took off into the sky again, and when it turned back at me, it inhaled a deep breath and spit a gout of black flame down at me, engulfing my entire body.

My armor shined brightly, and when the flame died back, I stood there, undamaged, smoking from the residual heat. The Dragon reared, taken aback, but did not stop its assault, diving down with its terrifyingly long claws pointed at me. I turned, sprinted back, and dove at the last second, skidding on my chestplate as the Dragon's claws just barely missed catching my armor. As it swooped back up, I flicked my bow into my hands and fired an arrow.

The shaft sped like a lightning bolt at the Dragon and struck it in the underbelly, bursting into flame when it struck. As if it were already on its way, the purple energy from another crystal washed over it, and it instantly went out, healing the damage that was done.

I turned my attention on the crystals. If I can't harm the Dragon because the crystals keep healing it . . .

I sped an arrow toward the closest crystal. When it struck, the crystal exploded, shattering into millions of tiny shards that rained down like a firework. The Dragon roared savagely.

"Found your secret," I growled and turned to fire again.

Another gout of black flame hurtled through the air at me. I knew that my armor was enchanted to protect against fire, but I did not know for how long that would be true, so this time I abandoned that shot, letting the arrow go wide off the crystal, and dove to the side. The fire washed over my leg, and I could feel it get a little hot. With normal fire, my armor could last perhaps all day every day, but fire from the dark god of the under realm? I'm not sure what kind of magic could hold up to that indefinitely.

The dragon reared up and screeched loudly. "*YOU WILL NOT DEFEAT ME!*"

I smirked. That was the key phrase. It meant I was already on my way to doing so. I counted quickly how many crystals were left—six! I could take care of six more crystals, if I was lucky. Then, and only then, would the fight become leveled.

I ducked behind the pillar of the one I shot. From that vantage, I could hit perhaps two more, if my aim was good and I was extremely lucky. Time to test my luck, I thought. I launched another arrow at the nearest crystal, and then immediately took off running to avoid the Dragon's incoming swoop. The arrow flew true—and bang! The crystal shattered into dust. Five to go.

The Dragon seemed to be getting more desperate. It flew high up and then turned back toward the ground, where it barreled straight down toward me. I had very little choice but to bolt to one side. The Dragon's gigantic mass crashed *through* the stone, leaving a huge crater. I heard it below the island. Now was my chance!

I dropped my bag, kicked the bottom of it. The nine diamonds scattered out of the bag and, behind them, the Wither Star. As quickly as I could manage, I stomped the nine diamonds into the ground, in the square pattern like the book had said. Then, I hefted up the Star and crashed it down on top of the center diamond. Instantly, a pillar of light shot up from the star, and I felt my body warm up a few degrees. The muscle strain of leaping and rolling and dodging slowly dissipated. Perfect.

Just as the pillar of light appeared, so too again did the Dragon over the side of the island.

No more words this time, the Dragon's eyes locked on the pillar, then on me. It opened its mouth again, but before it could spit more fire, I planted an arrow in its throat. It gurgled and screamed as the arrow burst into flames on contact, and as the crystal began to pump its energy into the Dragon, I let fly another arrow at that crystal.

"Oh, no, you don't!" I cried, and the arrow struck true. This time, though, the beam of purple energy faltered and shook and seemed to become ragged. The Dragon convulsed. Four to go.

I took this as an opportunity to dash toward the remaining towers and shoot down the crystals. Three, two . . .

I put my last arrow on the string and took aim at the final crystal. Just as the string left my fingers, though, I felt a searing pain crash through my nervous system and felt my body rise up off the ground. My fingers lost their grip on the bow, and I watched the last arrow I had fly wildly off course, off the edge of the island, and into the awaiting void. I crashed messily into the ground, and skidded several meters. When I tried to push myself back to my feet, I found that the Dragon's earth-shattering attack had broken my armor on my left arm and had broken the arm under it. I could barely even move my fingers, let alone hold up a bow.

Struggling to my feet, the Dragon loomed up over me.

"*Your little PLAN has come to its end, impudent little hero . . . You thought to destroy ME, the very GOD of this world? You FOOL! You shall die here and now, and not a soul alive will remember your passing! NOT A SOUL ALIVE—DO YOU HEAR ME?*" it screamed, its voice bordering on insane. I reared back, swung back its great claw. I pulled the sword out of my belt and held it with my one hand in front of me. This was the end. I tried; I tried, but it wasn't enough. The claw started to swing toward me. It would knock me off the island, into the void, and I would plummet for the rest of eternity. I shut my eyes.

Just then, I heard the sound of a miracle.

"Hands off, asshole!"

I opened my eyes to see Austin, Mary, Anne, Katy, and James, all standing on the edge of the plateau, all with arrows trained on the dragon. All at once, five arrows sliced through the air and planted themselves into the Dragon's breast. Its swing went wide and missed me. I swore and snapped my fingers.

"Man, is it good to see you! Shoot the crystal! Do it!" I shouted and sprinted. I could feel my arm already setting itself, thanks to the light of the beacon. Without its regenerative capability, I surely would have been killed on impact before.

Austin and Katy hurriedly dumped a bag of something that looked like a gray, stick sand on the stone. Quickly, they sculpted it into a T-shape, even as the others all aimed and fired at the last crystal. When it shattered, a wave passed through all of us, and the Dragon physically reduced in size by a considerable amount, as though the magic that was bolstering it was gone.

"*No, no! No! NO! IMPOSSIBLE!*" shouted the weakened Dragon, as it took in what was happening. All of its healing crystals were gone, and three black skulls had just been set on top of the pillar of sticky sand, and a low rumble was beginning to sound through the void.

That was all I needed. Mustering all my strength, I turned the blade downward and leapt onto the Dragon's back, plunging the blade to the very hilt in the dragon's back. At that moment, the telltale explosion of the Wither appearing rocked the floating island.

"*YOUUUUUU!*" hissed the Wither. The injured Dragon could only roar in return. I left the sword in the Dragon's back, dove off, and ran as fast as I could away from the Dragon, the Wither whizzing past me. The six of us watched as the two titans began to fight, old enemies fighting an old fight to change an old outcome.

Back in the Tetrapus, the fat book rotated slowly over our own enchanting table, which was now surrounded by shelves and shelves of books from another part of the library that the book had not been able to reach. Through the glass ceiling of the central hub, the pillar of light shone brightly. All six of us lounged lazily on the wool couches and beds in the communal quarters.

Far at the end of the Art wing, a thick glass case held two dark-colored objects: a thick, black skull and a round, grey egg. The title of the piece was, "The Death of the Gods." I like to think that their remains are still falling in that void, but then, we'll never really know. The book said that the End was sealed away forever once the Dragon had died. Sure, there would still be monsters and things to come to prey on us. That would likely never stop. The Dragon's influence on the world and the constant threat of the Wither, however?

Six brave heroes put a stop to that, one day long ago.

###